8-6

W9-ACR-671

The Zook Family Revisited Series

Book Two

Bitter Crossroad

by

June Bryan Belfie

JUNE BRYAN BELFIE

Other books by June Bryan Belfie

All About Grace
Inn Sane—Memoirs of an Innkeeper
A Long Way to Go—Historical fiction

The Zook Sisters of Lancaster County Series:
Ruth's Dilemma—Book One
Emma's Choice—Book Two
Katie's Discovery—Book Three

The Zooks Revisited Series
Waiting for Belinda—Book One

E-books:
Moving On
A Special Blessing for Sara
The Inn Game
(Above books available in paper Feb. 2014)

The Landlord

Copyright 2013
by June Bryan Belfie

All rights reserved. Except for the use in any review,
the reproduction or utilization of this work
in part or in whole is forbidden
unless permission is granted by the author..

This is a work of fiction.
All names and characters are from
the imagination of the author

I'd like to dedicate this book to my daughter, Lauren Boorujy, who encourages and prays for me as I write my novels. Her own struggles, which she has faced with unfaltering faith, are examples to all who know her. Often, I think of her as I write and instill her devotion to Christ in my characters. Thank you, Laurie. You are a blessing.

Be joyful in hope,
Patient in affliction,
Faithful in prayer

Romans 12:12 NIV.

Chapter One

As Belinda and Jeff drove closer to their destination in Ohio, her fears mounted. What would be her parents' response to this latest episode? Her desire to 'just have fun' had certainly created a mountain of trouble. Little had she known when she attended her friend's party in Pennsylvania that it would include pot smoking. If she'd known, she never would have gone. But would her parents believe her? After all, she'd gotten into difficulty earlier with her partying. Maybe if that were all she had done, her parents wouldn't have sent her away to stay with her aunt and uncle in Lancaster County. Things really got heated when they found out she sneaked off at night sometimes. How childish of her. Yah, she'd definitely matured these last few months. The English world was not her world. Never was—never would be. That was for sure and for certain.

She looked over and studied Jeff's profile as he concentrated on his driving. Traffic was heavy as they neared another urban area. He stared straight ahead, but his emerging smile told her he was aware of her glance. His right hand moved over to reach hers and she offered it, enjoying the warmth and gentleness of his touch. His blonde hair was even lighter than her own. He could have passed for her brother, though his blue eyes were more brilliant than her own green eyes.

"You okay?" he asked.

"I guess. I'm nervous about seeing my family again. I hope my daed isn't too upset still."

"I'd expect they'd probably ground you for awhile, but I hope not."

"Jah. I'm used to that. Actually, I'm more concerned about Nellie. My little sister's always looked up to me and I've sure failed as a role model."

"Don't be too hard on yourself. Maybe you got a little carried away during your *Rumspringa*, but you haven't done anything that bad."

"Nellie thinks I did. She knows I drank a couple times."

"She'll get over it, Belinda. She'll be sixteen next year, so she'll be tested herself."

"Nellie thinks more like my older sister. Rachel never did anything wrong. She was perfectly content to stay home and be a *gut* girl. I've really missed her. I hope she and Reuben aren't too upset about losing their first *boppli*."

"I saw her at your folk's house one time when I stopped by. She looked good. She's young and I'm sure they'll have other babies."

"Still, it doesn't make up for their loss."

"No, but it will help, don't you think?"

"Jah. Of course. Do you want a big family, Jeff?"

"As many as you want." His grin dimpled his chin and he took a quick glance in her direction. "After all, women do all the work."

"Jah, that's true. I think I'd like at least six, but we'll let the gut Lord determine it."

"You're gonna miss your Aunt Emma's twins, aren't you?"

"Oh, jah. They were ever so much fun. Cute as kittens."

Jeff laughed. "Say, are you getting hungry? We're coming up to an exit."

"I could eat something, though my tummy's been jumping around from all the stress."

"I'm sorry, Belinda. Try not to worry too much." He placed his hand back on the steering wheel and put his right signal on. They pulled into a McDonald's and walked around the perimeter for a couple of minutes to stretch before heading inside. After ordering and receiving their meals, they sat by a window and bowed their heads in silent prayer before eating. Belinda had fries and a milkshake, while Jeff worked on a Big Mac and coffee. She looked over at him as she sipped her shake. He was staring at her. "What's wrong?"

"Absolutely nothing. I can't believe you feel the same way I do. I hoped, but never suspected you loved me."

"You're very easy to love," she said, pushing the half empty container to the side. "I didn't realize how much I cared until lately. I wondered why I thought about you so much. Even when I was at Dawn's place, I compared you to every other guy and you always came out on top. I guess I was slow to figure out my feelings."

"Maybe you didn't want to love me, since I'm not Amish."

"Maybe."

"Do you think your family will understand if you become a Mennonite? After all, they aren't that different."

"It's probably going to come as a shock to them, but in time, I think they'll be okay with it. I don't want to tell anyone yet how we feel about each other, Jeff. I have to get through this other stuff first."

"I understand." He wiped his mouth and laid the tray to the side of the table. "Take as much time as you need. Should we discuss a date yet?"

"It's too soon. I hope it won't be long, but we have to be careful to keep our plans quiet."

"I know. I haven't even told my parents about changing over to the Mennonite religion yet."

"Will that be a problem?"

"I don't think so, but my father kind of makes fun of the way the men dress."

"Hmm. What would he say about me?"

"What could he say? You look adorable. I like you better in your Amish clothes than Carrie's outfits, even though you were a knockout."

Belinda laughed. "Oh, my, I thought I'd die the night I wore her mini skirt. I felt naked."

"My sister wears some pretty wild attire sometimes. Even my father made her change one day before she went out."

"Jeff, I hope you can stop by often once we're back. I'll miss you something fierce if I don't see you."

"I'll come as often as I can, without making it too obvious. You know your father and I enjoy our conversations about farming. I think we're learning a lot from each other."

"You're so smart. Are you definitely going to school in the fall?"

"I'm gonna take night classes so I can continue to work. I need the money, especially now that I plan to get married. I want to buy a small place with a couple acres."

"We may have to go out of the area a little. Land is getting expensive."

"True. It's the same in Lancaster County. I was talking to Emma's husband Gabe about it. Lucky he already has enough land."

"Jah. You can see why some Amish guys have to take manufacturing jobs with the English. There's just so much land to go around and with big families..."

He nodded. "I guess we'd better get back on the road. We still have a hundred miles to go."

"You must be exhausted, having driven to Pennsylvania this morning. I wish I could help out and drive a little."

He grinned. "That would be a sight—an Amish *maed* driving a car."

They walked hand-in-hand back to his vehicle and began the final leg of their trip.

Holmes County, Ohio

"Grace, stop pacing. They'll be here soon enough," Belinda's father, Jed, said to his wife. "Come on and sit with me while I drink my *kaffe*."

"Jah, well, I guess my wearing out the rug won't get my *dochder* here any faster, will it?" She sighed as she took a seat in the rocker across from her husband. "What are we going to say to her? I'm nervous. I don't want her to feel..."

"I know, I know. Unwanted. But we need to punish her for her behavior. You know that."

"I do know it and whatever you decide, you know I'll agree. I guess we can make her take on extra jobs like we did before she left."

"Jah. And keep her on the farm awhile till she changes her willful ways."

11

"I hope it will be soon. She's makin' an old lady out of me."

"Nee. You still look like you did the day I married you." Jed reached across and patted her knee.

Smiling weakly, she added, "I still want a nice supper tonight for them when they arrive. I bet they'll be real hungry."

"And tired. Jeff had to leave early this morning. Poor guy's been driving all day. Hope they don't have too much traffic to deal with."

"I hope he's a gut driver."

"He is. You rode with him. He's real careful. I felt perfectly safe with him."

"Jed, do you think they're sweet on each other?"

Jed cracked his first smile of the afternoon. "It wouldn't surprise me."

"You don't sound worried. Goodness, do you want our Belinda to leave the Amish community?"

"Nee, of course not, but maybe we can make an Amish man out of Jeff. We've had some long talks you know, and the boy's interested in the plain life."

"This plain?"

"He's got a Mennonite friend and he's mentioned going to the meetinghouse with him."

"Still ain't Amish."

"True Grace, but he's headed in the right direction, nee? If he yanks over, Belinda could do a lot worse. He's a hard worker and honest."

"Now how do you know that?"

"In my gut, that's how. You know I ain't often wrong about a man's character."

"You were once."

"Don't bring it up. It was a long time ago."

"Jah, but we were a hundred dollars poorer because of it." She grinned over at him as he pouted.

"Maybe someday we'll see that hundred again. After all, he's a cousin and he ain't dead yet."

"It was twenty years ago. I've written it off in my head."

"Jah?" He laughed heartily. "Except to remind me every so often."

Grace pulled back her smile and shook her head. "I'm scared she's going to leave the Amish if she falls for Jeff. It would break my heart, Jed."

"I'll talk to the bishop if it starts to look serious, honey. He's more modern and a lot faster in his thinking. Maybe it wouldn't mean banning."

"Mercy, I'd hope not! You wouldn't object to Belinda and Jeff getting married if it was okayed by the bishop? Even if he ain't turned Amish?"

"I look at it this way. It's gonna take a strong man to keep that girl in her place, and I think Jeff just might be that man. Time will tell. Right now we have to decide about her punishment."

"Gabe said she was a wonderful help while she was staying with them. Emma couldn't have managed all by herself right after having twins. Not with the other two *kinner* to take care of, too." Grace took a sip from her husband's coffee cup and settled back into the rocker.

"Jah, that young woman took a big bite when she married your brother and agreed to mother his two little ones. Gut thing she's quite a bit younger than he is."

"Pretty girl, too. All the Zook girls are nice to look at. That Katie is sweet. Takes real special care of her *grossmammi.*"

"She does. Hope our family is as concerned when we reach that age. After all, we need to look after our own."

Grace wiped her mouth with a tissue. "I'm gonna check Belinda's room. Make sure her bed is smooth."

"You're a gut mudder. Always thinking of your chicks."

She smiled over. "You ain't such a bad *daed* yourself. I'm making pot pie for later.""

"The prodigal son?"

"Maybe, something like that."

"Set a place for Jeff. It's the least we can do for him. He refused to take any money."

"Hmm. I'm still not sure how I feel about those two. I heard tell that Rebecca Smucker's nineteen-year-old brother Zeke has a fancy for Belinda. Maybe we should encourage that relationship, Jed. He's a hard-working young man and we've known the Smucker family for years."

"When cupid bites, it don't matter what we say. And I think Belinda's bit."

Grace grinned. "Same one that bit you a few years back?"

"Yah, and I'm still payin' for it." He rose, picked up his cup and winked at his wife, who shook her head and giggled.

Chapter Two
Lancaster County, Pennsylvania

Katie lugged her grandmother's bed sheets down the basement steps to be washed in the wringer washer. It was the third night in a row that Oma lost control and wet the bed. She had been so embarrassed, though Katie and her mother, Mary, had assured her it was not important and she needn't fret. Good thing Katie had laid plastic down under the sheets even before her grandmother returned from the nursing home, following her hip surgery. The nurses had warned there could be problems.

Katie placed the sheets and towels in the washer and stood watching as it filled with water. The tumbling water dulled her senses. Her depression.

It had been three days since she'd seen Josiah Stoltz. Surely, he wasn't losing interest in her. He was pleasant when he did show up, but it seemed he spent less time with her at each visit. He had stopped working on their house, since it looked like they wouldn't be living there after their wedding, due to her need to remain at home to help with Oma's care.

Katie stood, arms folded, watching the propane-driven washer, tug the linens back and forth—back and forth—just like her mind. One minute she longed to see Josiah; the next, she was almost relieved not to have him stop by. The emotional distance between them confused her, leaving her bordering on panic. Maybe it was better when she was too busy to worry about their relationship.

Maybe. Maybe not.

After a few minutes, Katie made her way up the stairs, holding the rail as she ascended. She'd definitely go to bed early tonight. What a day.

Her mother was peeling potatoes at the sink and looked over. "Katie, you look so tired. Go take a nap."

"Nee. Then I have a hard time sleeping at night. Maybe I'll just sit a few minutes before I put on new sheets."

"I already made up the bed. You relax now. Smell the brownies? They should be out in a few minutes and you can have one still warm, just the way you love them."

"The way I *used* to love them, Mamm. I don't have much appetite any more."

"You're gettin' way too thin, Katie. I hope you're not still dieting."

Katie shook her head. "I haven't worried about that for a few months now. Josiah says he likes me just the way I am."

"I think you've lost more weight. Check it later, dear. I can make French toast for your breakfast tomorrow. We have fresh maple syrup."

"*Danki.* That sounds gut."

Mary removed the brownies from the oven and tested one with a knife. "Perfect."

"Katie, Mary," Oma sang out from her room. "I smell something gut. What did you make now?"

"Brownies," Mary called back. "I'll bring you one when they cool off a little."

"Mamm," Katie remarked, "you look pretty worn out yourself. I'll take one into Oma when they're cool enough. Why don't you rest?"

"All right. I'd appreciate that. Did I tell you your Aunt Esther is coming in from Philadelphia next week-end?"

"Nee. That's nice. Are you glad?"

Mary reached for a rack and set the hot brownie pan on top. Then she turned, leaned against the counter and folded her hands in front of her. "Truthfully, I wish she'd wait a few more weeks. I'm not looking forward to having more houseguests right now. With Belinda back home, it's put more work on us and I'm really tired by bedtime."

"Aunt Esther would help, but you always tell her not to."

"Do I? I guess I do. Well, this time, I'll let her pitch in. She can even cook for us, if she knows how."

"Goodness, doesn't every woman?"

"She ate out a lot before she married Martin. She told me herself that cooking is last on her list."

"She's so rich, they probably still eat out a lot."

"Jah, I bet you're right. Oh, well, she can help clean up anyway. I don't think this kitchen would like three women all at the same time."

Katie laughed. "I told Emma I'd try to get over later to help with the twins, but I'm too tired. Think she'll be upset?"

"Nee. Wayne can ride over to tell her. You're pale, too, Katie. Maybe you should see the doctor."

"I'm not sick. Just tired."

"Very well." Mary reached for some small plates and cut the brownies in hearty-sized pieces. She placed the first one on a dish and handed it to Katie for Oma. "Here, ask Mamm if she wants some tea. I have the kettle on."

Katie came back and shook her head. "She wants a glass of milk instead. Only half a glass. I think she's afraid of wetting the bed if she has tea."

"Oh, poor dear. I feel so bad for her. Goodness, it's not important. Lots of old people have problems."

"I know. I tried to tell her it was okay, but she had tears, Mamm. I didn't know what to say."

Mary sighed. "You tried your best. Want to call Wayne? He and Daed are working the first field. The sweet corn is tasseling."

"We should help them, Mamm."

"Katie, we have too much to do this year. I'm just getting over my bronchitis and look how tired you are. Nee, they'll have to manage. Actually, your older brothers said they'd help when they have a chance sometime this week. Oh, and Mervin may help out, too. I think the boy likes to get away from the twins. He told Daed they cry a lot."

"Ach. Bet Lizzy doesn't mind. She's probably a big help to her parents. I love that little girl. I hope I have a child like her someday."

"She is a cutie pie. Emma's fortunate to have such nice kinner."

"Josiah said he wants at least six *boppli*. I hope we'll be as happy as Gabe and Emma. They're perfect for each other."

"Jah, they are. Is Josiah stopping by later?"

Katie looked down at her brownie and cut off a small piece with her fork. "He said he'd try."

"Katie, is anything wrong between you? You don't seem as happy as you were."

"We're fine. I think."

"Think?"

"Mamm, don't worry. Every couple has ups and downs."

"I suppose. He knows he's always welcome here, doesn't he?"

"Jah, I'm sure he knows that. You've always been real nice to him. Even when he used to come see Ruthie. And then Emma."

"Honey, does it bother you that he showed interest in your sisters before you?"

"Not too much. Maybe a little. Like, was I just a consolation prize?"

"Mercy. What a thing to say. His eyes light up every time he sees you."

Katie looked over at her mother. "Really? You're not just saying that?"

"Nee. I wouldn't lie, Katie."

"Does he still look at me like that?"

"Sure. Stop worrying, *dochder*. Things have been difficult with Oma and all. Of course, you're bound to feel a strain. And then with Belinda here, you and Josiah didn't have much chance to talk private-like."

"That's true. Maybe now, it'll be easier." Katie smiled over at her mother. "You always make me feel better, Mamm."

Katie's father, Leroy, came through the back door to the kitchen with his son, Wayne. "My goodness, I could smell those brownies from the fence."

Wayne walked over to the sink and washed his hands. "Gimme two, Mamm."

"Please?"

"Jah, please."

Leroy moved over to the sink next to his son and then rinsed off his own hands.

Wayne glanced over at his sister. "So Katie, where's your boyfriend these days?"

Katie's neck turned bright red. "Busy, I guess."

"Too busy to see you?" Wayne asked, a grin spreading across his face.

"Don't look so happy."

"I thought you two were like Romeo and Juliet."

19

Mary glared at her son. "Stop teasing your sister, Wayne."

"Jah, grow up, *brudder*," Katie added. Oh, she couldn't wait to have her own home. Of course, she loved her family, but there was no privacy. Everyone knew everything about her life. Hopefully, Oma would be well enough for her mother to handle her by late fall. She and Josiah had discussed the wedding date and he had left it all up to her. Perhaps January. It would be nice to be married by Christmas, though. Even if they had to stay in the *dawdi haus* attached to her parents' home, they'd have some space to themselves. If it was going to happen at all. Why did she think that way? Doubts kept creeping into her mind at the least expected moments. She found it suddenly difficult to breathe. Was this what it meant to have a panic attack? She panted several times till she felt normal again. Maybe a few extra hours sleep and her mood would improve.

"I hear a buggy coming," Katie said. "It looks like Josiah. Katie's heart leapt as she set her brownie aside to open the door. When Josiah appeared, he looked wonderful to her. His smile was engaging. He was the man she loved. Why so many misgivings? *Lord, what's wrong with me?*

Chapter Three
Holmes County, Ohio

"Here they come," Nellie called out as she ran into the kitchen from the yard. Without further ado, she ran back out and made her way over to Belinda and Jeff, who parked next to the barn.

Belinda grabbed her little sister and held her close. "I missed you tons," she said as Nellie patted her back.

"Me, too. It seems you've been gone forever." She pulled back and smiled over at Jeff who stood watching, as he held Belinda's suitcase by the handle.

"Hey, Nellie, what's up?"

"Not much, Jeff. Just you guys. Boy I bet you're gonna get it, Belinda. Daed's face was like a beet when he told us what you did."

"Oh, great. Is he in the house?"

"Jah. Waiting. Anything for me to carry?"

"You can get your sister's shawl in the back seat and the bag with food," Jeff said.

Belinda walked slowly toward the back door—the one she used to sneak out of in her bad days. It brought back some pretty nasty memories. Grace opened the screen and walked out to the back stoop. Mother and daughter embraced. "Come on in you two. You must be real tired."

Jeff nodded and gave her a smile. "Tired of being on the road, anyway. I don't like highway driving. You can't look at the scenery that much."

21

"It was a beautiful drive, Mamm. Where's Daed?"

"He went upstairs to change his shirt. He'll be down in a minute. Hungry?"

"I am," Jeff answered for Belinda. "Oops, I guess that wasn't meant for me."

Grace smiled. "It was meant for both of you. You'll stay and eat with us, Jeff? I made chicken pot pie."

"Thanks. I'd love to."

"I thought I smelled pot pie, Mamm. It smells so wonderful-gut in here. No one makes it like you do."

Grace puffed up her chest ever so slightly. "Well I don't know about that. Nellie made the apple pudding."

Belinda looked over as Nellie placed the *toot* of food on the counter and laid her sister's shawl over a chair. "Just the way you like it with lots of cinnamon," Nellie informed them.

Belinda heard her father's steps as he came down the stairs. Her stomach did a somersault and she licked her lips. What should she do? Hug him first? Or was he too upset with her to accept her affection? She worried for nothing, since he came right over and took her in his arms. "Oh, Daed, I'm so sorry I upset you again."

"Jah, well. We can talk later about that. Right now, you and Jeff should relax." He turned to Jeff and extended his hand, which Jeff shook. "Bet you're glad to be here after that long ride."

"I confess, I'm a bit sick of driving."

Gideon came in from the barn to greet his sister. He nodded and gave a slight smile.

"That's not much of a *hallo*," Belinda said, reaching over for an embrace.

He gave her a perfunctory hug, shook Jeff's hand and went to the stove, where he peeked in the oven. "Thought I smelled your pot pies, Mamm. Made extra I hope."

22

"I always make plenty, don't you worry. Take your *schwester's* suitcase up and lay it on her bed, *sohn,"* Grace said. "So tell us all about Oma. How is she doing?"

"Improving, I guess. She still needs a lot of care, but *Aenti* Mary is feeling better now and of course, Katie's there to help."

"You think they were upset you were coming home?" Grace asked.

"Nee, I think they'll be fine. I miss the little twins though. It was a lot more fun when I was staying with *Onkel* Gabe and *Aenti* Emma. Their little Lizzy was a sweetheart, too. Though I won't miss her funny noises at night. Sometimes she even snored."

Grace laughed. "We'll see everyone again when Katie gets married. I promised the family we'd come out for the big occasion."

"I'd be surprised if the wedding takes place this fall. Maybe after Christmas. Katie said as much to me the other day. Her *grossmammi* still needs nursing care. I feel sorry for Katie, though she acted like it wasn't a big deal. I was surprised."

Grace turned to Jeff. "Do you want to sit down and relax before we eat?"

"I've been sitting so long, I think I'll go for a walk around the property instead. Wanna go with me, Gideon?"

"Nee, I have to go back and milk the cows."

"Want help?"

"Ever milk?"

"A couple times."

"Okay. Come on."

Belinda looked over at Jeff and smiled. "Remember you asked for it."

After they left the house, her father followed them out to the barn and Belinda went up to unpack her suitcase. Her room looked ever so inviting. Nee, it wasn't fancy like her English friends' bedrooms, but she patted her pillow and looked out the window at the all too familiar landscape. Even though it was late August and things looked dry from lack of rain, it was home. Her home. And she hoped she'd never have to leave Ohio again.

After dinner, she walked Jeff out to his car. Nellie tagged along and Belinda wondered if it was per chance or per instruction from her parents. Either way, it left no opportunity for her to be alone with Jeff. He touched her arm once with his hand and mentioned he'd try to come by in a couple of days, and then he was off. While she watched his car turn at the road, Nellie pulled on her apron. "What, Nellie?"

"Just wondered if you guys are in love."

Belinda's mouth dropped open. "Why would you ask that?"

"I think you are, that's why. He looks at you like you're the only one in the room and I see the way you smile back."

"Oh, Nellie, don't tell the folks, but we are in love."

"Wow! I knew it! Are you getting married?"

"We want to, but I know we're not of the same world."

"Daed said Jeff wants to be a Mennonite."

"It's true."

"How strict? Electricity and cars?"

"Jah. I think so. Black cars." They started walking back to the house.

"Do you want that?"

"If it's the only way we can get married, we could even skip the car bit. I don't really care one way or the other."

"I bet you'd like air-conditioning."

"Well, yah, who wouldn't?"

"I wouldn't care. I want to marry a regular Amish man. I love riding in buggies and the soft kero lighting we have in our homes. You can keep the new-fangled ways." When they reached the farmhouse, they sat on the back stoop next to a flower bed.

Belinda smiled over at her sister. "There's a lot to be said for that way of life. You'll make a gut Amish wife, that's for sure."

"Did the folks tell you how they're gonna punish you?"

"Not yet."

"I know what they plan. It's not that bad. In fact, it's pretty much what happened before you left. Just more work and you'll have to hang around here and not go out with your friends."

"I figured. I can handle it. I'm glad it's not worse. Nellie, I'm sorry I disappointed you."

Nellie picked an orange marigold and smoothed the stiff petals. "It's okay. I knew you'd come around."

Belinda let out a slow breath. "It took a policeman to make me realize how serious it was getting."

"Whoa! I didn't hear about that. What happened?"

"I was at a party with friends and it got loud and I guess a neighbor complained, but anyway, policemen barged in. They even arrested a couple kids."

"Were you scared?" Nellie's eyes were like ping-pong balls.

"Oh, jah. Terrified! They took my name and all and the next day came to report it to my aenti and onkel."

"Were the kids drinking?"

"More than that. They were smoking pot. I had no idea they'd be doing that. Believe me, I would never have gone there if I'd known."

"Did the family believe you?"

"I don't know. That's when we called Mamm and Daed. Never again. Those Englishers are gonna be sorry one day."

"They're losers, that's what they are." Nellie scowled and threw the marigold aside. "It's a gut thing you came home."

"I'm glad to be back. I missed everyone."

"What about Jeff? Did you tell him what happened?"

Belinda nodded. "He understood. He's wonderful, Nellie. So kind and sweet."

"Doesn't hurt that he's handsome."

Laughing, Belinda winked over. "No, that ain't a problem at all.

Chapter Four
Lancaster County, Pennsylvania

Josiah waved to Katie's father and brother as he parked his buggy near the Zook's barn. Coming through the kitchen door, he removed his straw hat and placed it on a knob by the door. "How's my Katie today?"

Katie grinned over as she wiped her hands on a dishcloth. "Gut. Better now that you're here. It's been a hard day."

His brows rose. "Harder than others?"

"Jah. I can explain later. Right now, I need to set the table."

"Can I help?"

"Nee. Just keep me company."

Mary greeted him as she came into the kitchen to check the roast and then he poked his head into Oma's room to say hello.

As he sat on a kitchen chair to watch Katie, she scooted about the kitchen, preparing the rest of the meal.

Once the preparations were complete, the young couple took a few minutes for themselves and walked around the yard. They stopped by his buggy while Josiah took the harness off his mare. Katie watched as he led the animal to the corral.

"My Katie looks tired. Aren't you getting enough sleep?"

"I guess I am, but I wake up sometimes in a horrible sweat. It takes me awhile to get back to sleep."

"Huh. What does your mamm say about that?"

"I haven't mentioned it. She's got enough on her mind with Oma and all. Have you done any more work on our house?"

"Nee. I've been too busy at my job. By evening, I'm beat. Oh, I went to an auction Saturday and picked up some farm equipment real cheap. They all need work, so I've been fixing them up, hopefully in time to make hay for the winter. Did I tell you I'm staying at the house all the time now?"

She shook her head. "I thought you wanted to wait till we married." She tried to hide her disappointment. After all, it was supposed to be *their* home, not just his.

"I was gonna wait, but it's too tight at home. It's not fair to my mamm and daed, so I decided to move over there. I like it even though I have a lot of work to do yet."

"I guess there's no hurry." She felt a pang of sorrow, realizing it could be quite awhile before she'd be his wife. Katie watched the cows head over toward the fence, knowing from habit it would soon be time to be milked. Their bags were bulging.

"Katie, you look so sad. Time will pass quickly and someday we'll be together all the time."

"Sometimes, I wonder if it will really happen."

"Honey, of course it will. You're not having a change of heart, are you?"

She looked into his eyes. "Not me, but I wonder sometimes how you feel."

"Why would you say that?"

"You don't stop by everyday the way you used to, for one thing."

"Katie, I've been busy. I just told you. Besides, when I do come, you're always fussing with your grossmammi or cooking or something that doesn't involve me. Tell you the truth, it doesn't seem you have much time for me anymore. Did you ever think of my feelings?" His voice was raised, and she'd never seen him look as angry. Perhaps her worst fears were true.

"Can I help it if I'm needed?" she said in her defense. "What would you have me do? Run out and leave Oma alone? Don't forget my mamm has been sick a lot."

"She's all better now, and you still don't seem to have time for me. I can take a hint, Katie. I don't need a bulletin in *The Budget.*"

"I'm sorry you feel you've been neglected. That's a bit childish, don't you think?" Katie said, eyes glistening.

"Oh, so now I'm being childish! Katie, what's gotten into you?"

She allowed her tears to flow and he placed his arms around her. "Katie, do you want to talk?"

"Nee. I don't know. Maybe I'm just tired. Please don't listen to me anymore. I don't even mean what I say."

He moved back and wiped her cheek with his hand. "It's not like my happy Katie to be so upset. Don't your *schwesters* ever come to help?"

"Emma can't really come now that she has the twins to take care of. Plus her other two. Ruthie stops frequently, but it's hard for her with a boppli and expecting and all. Usually, we can manage okay, but Oma doesn't seem to be trying too hard to improve."

"Jah, well, she is old and between the accident and the hip surgery, she's been through a lot."

"The worst was losing *grossdawdi.* She'd known him her whole life."

"They were real close, weren't they?"

"Jah. Real close. She says when he died it was like losing part of herself. Poor lady. I feel guilty for complaining. She's been through so much and she asks for so little."

"It's still hard on you. I know that. I hope you don't hurt your back lifting her like you do."

"So far, my back has been okay. If I could get my sleep at night..."

"Maybe you should drink warm milk before you go to bed. You're losing weight, too, aren't you, Katie?" He stood a couple feet back and scanned his eyes from her *kapped* head to her black leather shoes.

"I guess so. You're not changing your mind about me, are you, Josiah?"

He gave a low chuckle and grinned at her, taking her hands in his. "Nee. That's not going to happen, Miss Zook. I just heard the dinner bell. We'd better get back before your mamm gets upset."

They returned and Katie felt more assured of her future, though something continued to nag at her spirit, and the anxiety persisted in spite of his words.

That night, before she fell asleep, Katie prayed and asked God to protect their love for each other. She also asked for release from her misgivings and strength to handle her heavy responsibilities. Feeling calmer, she closed her eyes and fell off to sleep.

Holmes County, Ohio

Grace and Jed stood by their earlier decision to add chores to Belinda's already busy schedule. It was deemed necessary to show their daughter consequences for her past behavior. Belinda accepted the penalties, though she did not enjoy weeding by herself. Nellie appeared to avoid her older sister since she'd told her about the policeman. It was hurtful to Belinda, though it was nice to be back home in spite of the additional workload.

Memories of Jeff's confession of love continued to flood her mind and as she did the tedious chores handed to her, she was uplifted by the knowledge one day she would be married to this wonderful man. How could she have been so blind? It was obvious from the beginning they were attracted to each other.

Thinking back, she remembered how her heart had raced when he spoke to her and how she relied on him in most circumstances. He'd even come to her rescue when she found herself going too far with that handsome college student at one of Carrie's parties. Funny, she didn't even think about partying anymore. Oh, she hoped to dance again, but even if it never happened, it was not a big deal anymore. Nee, the big deal—the *biggest* deal—in her life was the fact she was engaged to marry. Not officially, perhaps, but secretly, and that was a lot more fun.

When she thought about announcing it to the family, she felt a pit, now the size of a grapefruit, swell inside. It would not be easy. Nee, how would her parents feel about her marrying someone outside the Amish community? Would they want to shun her? Probably Nellie would. Sweet Nellie. Oh, that would be horrid indeed. She'd certainly come around. Wouldn't she? Belinda pushed her bonnet off her head, moved under a maple tree for shade, and sat with her legs folded beneath her. It was hot for late August. She removed her bonnet and released her long blonde hair. A breeze send a chill down her back.

She looked down at her dirt-stained hands. Her nails were in 'mourning' as her mother called it when they became soiled from weeding. Thank goodness tomorrow was Gideon's thirteenth birthday and she'd see her friends, and best of all, Jeff. She'd been delighted when her father had asked him to attend the party when he left her off that evening. Would he have invited him if he'd known how they felt about each other? Surely not. It would have to remain a secret. They had not discussed their future beyond the fact that it would include a marriage. What would transpire between now and then?

Mercy. That was what they'd need. God's mercy and their family's as well.

Chapter Five
Holmes County, Ohio

Rachel and Reuben arrived at the house early to help with the preparations for the birthday party. Belinda hugged her older sister and they held each other for several extra seconds.

"Let me look at you," Belinda said, holding her at arm's length. "You look gut. How do you feel?"

"Better than before," Rachel said, a hint of sorrow still lodged in her words.

"I'm glad. I pray for you both every day."

Reuben, who had been standing back to allow the sisters their moment together, came forward and patted Belinda on the shoulder. "We felt the prayers of others. It was a real support for us. At least we know our little one is with the Lord."

"Jah, it helps, I'm certain of that."

Rachel appeared to force a smile. "So, where's the birthday boy?"

"In the field with daed. We told him to stay out until we call him. Nellie's blown up a dozen balloons, which we should stick on the ceiling. Reuben, we'll need you for that."

He grinned. "Jah, I can handle that job. Just don't make me ice the cake."

"Oh, that's done already. Mamm made his favorite. Chocolate with white icing."

Reuben stood on a stepstool and Rachel handed him the balloons along with tape, one at a time.

"Where's Nellie?" Rachel asked.

"She avoids me at all turns."

"Goodness. Why?"

"I guess she's ashamed of me. When I first came home, things seemed gut, but then after telling her what I did, well…"

"Oh, Belinda. That's ridiculous."

"Is it? I did bring shame on the family, the way I behaved."

"It's not like you committed a crime. I'll have a talk with her later. She's acting foolish-like."

"I don't know if it will help, but maybe if you try…"

"Are we setting up folding chairs?" Reuben asked. "How many people do you expect?"

"Mamm figured about forty, but I think there'll be more. According to Gideon, even some of my friends are coming."

"I guess everyone will bring something to eat."

"Jah, they always do," Belinda said with a grin. "What's in the bowl you brought in?"

"Three-bean salad. Daed always insists on me making it. I put in more soy sauce than most people."

"Jah, it's gut, that's for sure."

"I hear a buggy on the drive." Rachel poked her head out the kitchen door as a buggy turned the corner of the drive. "It looks like Rebecca Smucker and a couple of her brothers."

Belinda looked out, too. "Caleb and Zeke."

"I knew Caleb would come, since he and Gideon are such gut friends, but I wonder why Zeke is coming. He's nineteen, isn't he?" Rachel asked.

"Jah." Belinda knew why. Because she was here. She wouldn't hurt his feelings by ignoring him, but she wished he hadn't chosen to attend.

Reuben and the girls went out to greet them and Zeke pulled at his suspenders, his face taking on a reddish hue. "You look gut, Belinda. You glad to be home?"

"Jah, I am. I missed everyone."

Rebecca put her arms around Belinda and smiled broadly. "I missed you a lot."

Belinda nodded. "It was hard sometimes to be so far away."

"Where's Gideon?" asked Caleb.

"In the field behind the orchard. You can go get him to stop now, if you want. Just don't let him in the house yet."

Caleb took off and the others went back in the kitchen.

"Can I help?" Zeke asked.

"Not really," Belinda said.

"Why don't we get out of the way," Reuben said to Zeke. "We can get chairs from the barn and set them around. Outside or in?" he asked Belinda.

"Mostly outside." After directing him, she, Rachel, and Rebecca placed tablecloths on folding tables under two of the shade trees in the back yard. They returned to the kitchen for supplies as Nellie and her mother came down from upstairs. The women hugged each other and their laughter filled the room—already lit up from the colorful balloons and bright paper birthday decorations.

Belinda looked around her. Jah, it was gut to be home again.

By three o'clock, the house was spilling over with friends and family. Many of their guests were lounging under the shade trees, but Belinda worked in the kitchen with some of the other women, filling baskets and platters with food. She could hardly hear herself speak with all the laughter and hearty conversation. Every time the screen door opened, she looked over to see if it was Jeff, but he didn't arrive until nearly four.

By then she was sitting on the porch with several other friends, Zeke included. He had managed to sit beside her on the glider, much to her displeasure. He was nice enough, but he was beginning to push, asking her to attend a frolic with him the next day. She found several excuses, though they sounded hollow, even to her. Then she remembered she was grounded, and that seemed to satisfy him.

After Carrie and Jeff parked their car, Belinda rose and went to greet them, forcing herself not to run into his arms. He looked so handsome in his jeans and white cotton shirt. Jeff's skin was tan and his hair was nearly bleached white from the sun. He grinned when he spotted her.

After she and Carrie danced around hugging each other, she allowed him a "brotherly" hug. Their eyes exchanged far more than friendship, though no one else seemed to notice. Belinda introduced Carrie and Jeff to her other friends. When she got to Zeke, he held out his hand, but his mouth turned down. Amazing how competition finds itself without words. Belinda glanced at Jeff, who also had a frown. Goodness! Men!

"Quite a crowd," Jeff remarked, glancing around at the small groups of plain-dressed folks scattered about the yard.

"We have a big community," Zeke said, unsmiling.

Jeff nodded. "I'd have a hard time remembering everyone's name."

"When you grow up Amish, you don't have that problem. We look out for each other and you can count on your friends."

"Even though I'm English, we have our dependable friends, as well," Jeff said, defensively.

"Not like we do. I know the English. They can turn on each other very easy."

Belinda stepped into the conversation. "Let's get you something to eat, Jeff." She took hold of his arm and led him toward a picnic table laden with food. One of the children stood fanning the flies away with a paper fan.

"What's wrong with your friend?" he asked once they were out of hearing distance.

"Don't pay any attention to Zeke. He's just a grouch sometimes."

"I think he has his eyes on you, Belinda. You'd better watch out."

She laughed. "Mercy, he's not dangerous. Jah, he may like me a little, but not to worry, my dear. I only have eyes for you."

Jeff grinned at her and patted her cheek. "I'll watch over you."

"Just like you did with the other guys?"

"More so. Now you're mine."

"Shhh," she nodded toward the young girl keeping the flies away. "Little pitchers…"

Jeff laughed. He helped himself to a plateful of food and they walked together to an empty bench a few feet from the others. "Gideon's the center of attention. Look at the girls around him."

Belinda giggled. "Oh, jah, he's gonna be a heart-breaker."

"Like his sister?"

"He's always attracted the girls, even when he was ten. He pretends to be shy, but in reality, he's pretty self-confident."

"I've missed you," he said, softly. "I don't know how long we can wait before telling everyone."

"It won't be long. I just need to get through the next few weeks first. I don't want to add fuel to the fire by announcing my plans to leave the Amish for Mennonite."

"I still don't know why it would be a big deal."

"Maybe it won't be. The subject has never come up before and—"

Nellie called over to them. "Belinda, Mamm wants you to light the candles on the cake."

"I'll be there." She looked over at Jeff. "I guess they noticed I was walking away from the group. Naughty me."

He laughed. "Maybe you're the only one who knows how to light candles."

"Oh, jah. How true." She laughed and they turned to head back.

There was no other opportunity to be alone with Jeff and she watched later when he left with Carrie. How amazing that he loved her—a plain simple Amish girl like herself.

God was smiling upon her. Hopefully, her father on earth would be as happy.

Chapter Six
Lancaster County, Pennsylvania

Oma wrapped her arms around Katie's neck as she swung slowly around and placed her feet on the floor beside the bed. It took longer all the time to get her up from her bed. She insisted on walking to the bathroom, which Katie and her mother encouraged. It disturbed them both that the poor lady seemed weaker each passing day. She still wet the bed most nights, but they used adult diapers to save the bedding. Even with protection, Katie had to change the sheets nearly every day. It was taking a toll on her health. She was surprised at how exhausted she was every night even at her age.

"Mercy. I feel as wobbly as a new lamb," Oma stated as she slowly made her way to the bathroom, holding on to Katie with trembling hands.

"Take your time."

"I ain't got much of that," she said with a grin. "My bladder's mighty full, that's for sure."

After Katie helped her get seated, she stood outside the door to allow her privacy. Katie glanced out the window of the bedroom while she waited. It was beginning to rain again. The third day in a row. Funny, how it affected her spirit. Depression was something Katie had dealt with before, but since she and Josiah had fallen in love, she'd been relieved of the heavy cloud of sadness on her life. Why was it returning? Of course, she knew why, if she allowed herself to think about her whole situation. She loved her grandmother and wanted to be there to help, but it was exhausting. She had little time for Josiah, even when he did show up. Fear crept into her heart. Would there be a wedding after all? What kind of wife could she be when she felt so tired all the time and out of sorts. Even her mother had gotten annoyed the day before at her general attitude. Nee, it wasn't gut. She'd have to spend less time thinking about herself and more time trying to help her poor grandmother. Today, she'd sew with her—if Oma was up to it. For the past week, she'd only spent about a half hour on her quilting. That wasn't like her grandmother. She used to turn out a quilt every couple months. This one had been sitting on the frame for months. Of course, there was little incentive. Katie caught her grandmother crying more frequently as of late. The pain of separation from her husband after his tragic death in the buggy accident seemed to be increasing rather than diminishing with the passage of time. Would she and Josiah be as close someday as her grandparents had been?

"I'm done, Katie. You can help me back to bed now, sweetie."

Katie supported her grandmother with her arm and led her toward a chair. "The therapist wants you to sit up more. Why don't you rest while I get you something to eat? You didn't have much breakfast."

"Oh, I'm not hungry. I'll try to sit for a little while though. Maybe you can read to me."

"Jah, but first I have to check and see if the clothes are dry in the basement. This rain has made it difficult to keep up with the wash."

"It don't help to have me add to your load."

"Please don't worry about that. We all make dirty clothes." Katie helped Oma get seated and added a lap quilt, placing it over her grandmother's spindly legs. Then she placed a sweater around her shoulders and arms. The loose skin on her upper arms drooped, making her appear even thinner than she was.

Katie held onto the wooden railing as she descended the steps to the basement. She folded the dry sheets, but left the towels to dry more thoroughly. A clap of thunder startled her and the kerosene lamp dimmed as it began to run out of fuel. She found the can with kerosene and filled a different lamp for light. It took several matches before one worked. The humidity was so thick it could be cut with scissors.

Katie sighed. Why hadn't Josiah stopped by? It was three, no four, days since he'd come by to see her and he'd only stayed about an hour. Of course, she had been putting up tomatoes with her mother and they'd had no opportunity to spend time alone. She'd seen the look of disappointment on his face, but certainly he'd understood it wasn't by choice. A mature man would understand.

Katie lugged the dry sheets and clothes upstairs in the basket and laid it down in the kitchen. She'd put things away later, after she read to her grandmother. Her mother, Mary, was kneading bread and looked over at her. "Oma needs to drink some juice, Katie. She left most of her egg this morning."

"Jah, I know. She says she's not hungry."

"Ach. I'm worried about her. She has to eat more. She's as thin as a straw."

"You can't force her, Mamm. I'll take the juice in to her, but if she's not thirsty..."

"At least you can try."

"You don't think I try? I try all the time! That's about all I do! I *try* to take gut care of Oma."

"Katie. Katie. I didn't mean to hurt you. You do so much. Come here and give me a hug. I'm sorry you thought I was criticizing you."

Katie moved over to her mother's waiting arms and began to weep. "I'm just real tired, Mamm."

"Jah, I know, honey. We all are. It's not easy." She stroked her daughter's back with one hand and held her close with the other. "My poor *dochder*. You've never complained."

Katie pulled back slightly to look at her mother's expression. "I'm not a gut person. I think too much about myself."

"Hush, that's foolishness. You're a wonderful-gut girl. I don't know how I'd manage without you. Maybe Hannah can come give you a break."

"How can she with all her boppli? Nee, I'll be okay. Maybe when Oma takes a nap, I'll take one, too. I admit I'm awful tired lately."

"Katie, you're pale, too. Of course, you don't get much sun."

"What sun? I think the Lord has decided to take it away for a while. He seems to make wet all the time."

Mary reached for Katie's hands. "Jah, the rain is tiresome, that's for sure. But look at the corn. It's up to Daed's shoulders."

Katie dropped her mother's hands and reached for a tissue on the counter. "I need to go read now, Mamm. Oma's waiting. Danki for helping me."

"You're a gut girl. Josiah is a lucky young man."

Katie nodded and left the kitchen quickly before her mother had a chance to see the fresh tears forming in her eyes. That was a whole other issue.

Holmes County, Ohio

Jeff enjoyed college, though between attending classes, studying, and working days at his landscaping job, it left little time for visiting Belinda. It had been nearly a week since he'd dropped by to see her, and Nellie made quite a point of hanging around her sister every time he showed up. He found it annoying, but could think of no way to work around it. After all, he was just glad her parents still allowed him to stop by. Once he paid a visit with Carrie, but that left him less time with his Belinda. Even with everything going on in his life, he thought about her almost constantly.

She wouldn't let him take her picture, even after he begged her, but her lovely eyes and delicate beauty were permanently affixed in his mind.

It was time to tell his parents about his decision to become a Mennonite. He was pretty sure they'd be okay with it, but he had wanted to be sure of his own resolve before making the announcement. Carrie already knew and he had told her about his relationship with Belinda, though she was sworn to secrecy about their engagement. Belinda wanted to be sure her parents were the first to know, and it wasn't the right timing for that disclosure.

There was really no hurry, since he wanted to complete his education and get his business started before taking on the responsibility of a wife and family. It would be hard though. He loved Belinda so much and wanted to know the love and support of a wife. Still, he would be wise. She was very young and he wasn't much older. Belinda had matured since he first met her, but it wasn't long ago that she'd made some foolish choices. No, more time wasn't a bad thing. It gave them the ability to get to know each other. Of course, he'd like to spend more time with her alone. But he'd be content to just be in her presence. At least for now.

Sunday afternoon, instead of heading over to Belinda's, he stayed around the house. It had finally stopped raining. He and his father set up the grill and placed sirloin steaks over the burning coals. His mother made potato salad and Carrie husked corn. The family sat on the patio and ate together. It was pleasant and seemed like the right time to discuss his decision. When he was done talking, his father shoved his chair back and folded his arms.

"I can't say I'm surprised, son. You've only attended church once with the family all summer, so I figured you were seriously considering the Mennonite faith. Have you thought about how your friends will feel though, if you start wearing their style clothing and give up your nice car?"

"They'll understand and if they don't, well, there's nothing I can do about that. I have to follow my heart."

His mother's forehead wrinkled. "Are you doing this because of Belinda?"

His jaw dropped. "Belinda?"

"Jeff, it's obvious, you're interested in that girl. You've been attracted to her for a while now. I've seen how you look at her when she comes to our stand. And you went all the way to Pennsylvania to bring her back home."

"Well, we are good friends, but my decision to become Mennonite is my own."

"It wouldn't hurt to become plain, though, would it, if you were serious about Belinda?" She asked, raising one brow.

"Honestly, even if I'd never met her—"

"But you have." His mother frowned. "She's a strict Amish girl, Jeff. She'll never leave the Amish. Don't get yourself involved."

Carrie and Jeff exchanged glances. "We'll see, Mom. Don't worry about me. I can take care of myself."

"I just don't want you to get hurt. She's a lovely girl, but there are plenty of nice girls in your own circle of friends."

"If I become Mennonite, I'll have a whole new circle."

"True. Maybe you'll find a nice girl at your meeting house."

"Mmm. Well, I'm glad you both understand."

"Will you go the buggy route?" his father asked with his lips drawn.

"Probably not. I'd have a hard time getting to school. No, I'll turn in my car for a black one soon. And as far as my clothes go, I don't need to make many changes. I dress pretty plain even now."

Carrie laughed out loud. "You can't wear your bulky red sweater anymore. Can I have it?"

He turned and grinned. "It will swim on you?"

"That's the idea. I love it. It would look cool with my white jeans."

"Go for it. It was too hot for me anyway. When we're done here, I guess I'll go for a ride. Seems all I've done lately is study and work."

"Want me to go along?" Carrie asked, aware of his destination.

"That's okay." He smiled over and she winked at him.

After cleaning up, he changed into long pants and combed his blonde curls back away from his eyes. He couldn't wait to see Belinda and tell her about his discussion with his family. So it was obvious to everyone about his feelings. Perhaps even *her* parents were aware of their love. That was the next hurdle, but it would be Belinda's call and timing. He said a prayer and headed for his car.

Chapter Seven
Lancaster County, Pennsylvania

Katie looked at the calendar hanging in the kitchen. An entire week had passed and no word from Josiah. Where was he? Why hadn't he at least gotten word to her? Was he ill? Had he gotten bored with her? Was the marriage off?

Katie was close to tears all the time now. Her parents were concerned, though she tried to blame her emotional roller coaster ride on fatigue. Even her brother, Wayne, asked what was wrong with his sister.

Oma patted her hand after Katie helped her back in bed after doing some minor physical therapy with her. "Sweetie, it wonders me. You're not yourself lately."

"I'm fine. Just quiet, is all."

"Nee. More than that. Is it that young man you plan to marry? He ain't been here in a while now."

Katie sat in the rocker beside her grandmother's bed and leaned her head back against the wooden headrest. "I don't know what's wrong. He's never stayed away this long. I wish he had a phone. The bishop's allowing cell-phones now, you know."

"Jah. Strange business these magic phones. Maybe he should buy one?"

"I mentioned it once and he just laughed. Said he didn't want to be bothered with one."

47

"Well, we got along just fine all these years without them. Maybe he's right."

"I just hope he's not sick."

"Why don't you take the buggy and go check for yourself. I need to take a nap anyway and your mamm is around if I need anything."

"She's coughing more lately. I hope she's not getting sick again."

"Oh, my. That would not be gut. You go, though, *liebschen*. Please, for my sake. I don't want to be the reason for you to break up with your young man."

"Maybe I will go over. Jah, I'll check with Mamm first to be sure."

An hour later, Katie was on her way to the home where she had planned to spend the rest of her life. Her heart beat wildly as she directed the horse around the drive toward the back of the farmhouse. She spotted Josiah working on a piece of machinery next to the barn. He looked up when he heard the buggy wheels and waved to her. Her mouth was so dry, she was afraid she wouldn't be able to swallow. How would he react to her coming unannounced?

"Katie, what a nice surprise," he said as he came beside the buggy and reached for her hand. She climbed down and before she had a chance to say anything, he enveloped her with his arms. "Is everything okay?"

"Jah, I just wondered what you were doing. It's been a week since I saw you."

"I'm sorry. I was planning to stop by this afternoon. I just had to get this baler ready first. I've been working all week getting ready to harvest. You don't look well, Katie. Have you been sick?"

"Nee. Maybe a little sick with worry is all. I thought maybe you were ill and no one was here to watch after you."

"Danki for your concern. That was really nice of you. Come on in and I'll show you what I've been doing in the house. I still want to have it ready by winter for you. Just in case."

"Mmm. I don't know. It looks like our wedding may have to be postponed."

"Katie, we can live in the dawdi haus like your parents suggested. I don't mind."

"Maybe. I wanted to live in our own place, though." She felt her eyes tear up, but she forced a smile.

"I know." He took her hand and they walked through the kitchen door. "See? Do you like the cabinets? I painted them white, just like you wanted."

Katie dropped his hand and went over to one of the cupboards and opened the door. "Jah. They look real nice. Shiny."

"And look at the floor. I put in new vinyl. Do you like it?"

She looked down at the cobblestone design. "It's pretty. You did a gut job."

"You haven't seen anything yet. Come upstairs and I'll show you the bedrooms. I painted them all this past week at night. That's another reason I didn't get by to see you. I'm trying to get everything done."

Katie walked up the steps in front of him and then he took her by the hand and showed her the bedrooms. "I bought a double bed for our room. It's a pretty gut mattress." The bed was covered with one sheet and a loose quilt. Two pillows were scattered against the headboard. It looked as if he had problems sleeping himself.

Katie walked over and pushed down on the bed with her hand to test the softness. "Jah, it feels nice. Not too soft." She flushed when she realized it would one day be theirs to share. She quickly walked toward the door.

"And this will be the nursery," he said, as he walked toward the small bedroom at the end of the hallway. "I painted everything white, since I thought it would be easier that way. Saved on paint, too."

"It's bright. Even though it's cloudy out." As she headed toward the hallway again, Katie felt light-headed. She hadn't eaten lunch. Her hand automatically reached for the wall. She stood slightly slumped over and took long breaths, as she attempted to stabilize herself. Josiah reached for her waist and held her securely until she was able to take a step on her own.

"Katie, what's wrong?"

"I'm not sure, but I think I should have eaten lunch before I left the house. I'm kinda dizzy."

"Hold on to the wall. I have a straight chair in the bedroom." He walked quickly to retrieve it and set it beside her in the hall. "Here, sit until you feel better. Do you want a glass of water?"

"Jah, maybe."

He went into the bathroom and returned with a plastic glass filled with cool water. "Drink it slowly."

She sipped several times and then drew a long breath. "I feel better now. I started to black out and see spots. It was scary."

"Maybe you should see a doctor."

"Nee, I'm sure it was my empty stomach playing tricks on me. I'll be fine." She smiled up at him. "Danki. The house looks really gut, Josiah. I think I can go downstairs now." They headed for the stairwell, but before they descended, a female voice came trilling up the stairs.

"Josiah, where are you?" It sounded like Priscilla Miller, but what on earth would she be doing here? After all, she was getting married soon. Katie's heart sank as she looked over at Josiah. His expression was not only one of shock, but embarrassment as well. Explanations were in order.

Holmes County, Ohio

Nellie poked her head out the front door as she heard car wheels on the gravel drive. "Belinda, Jeff's here."

Belinda's heart raced as she smoothed her loose hairs, tucking them under her prayer kapp, and pinched her cheeks to encourage a blush. She and her mother were cutting apples to dry. Grace looked over at her daughter. "For just a friend, you seem mighty excited."

"Do I?" She took a deep breath and slowed her pace as she headed outside to greet him. Nellie was two steps behind. Turning and glaring at her sister, Belinda realized there was purpose behind Nellie's interest. She was spying. Action probably approved of by the head of the CIA—her father. My, it wasn't fun to be distrusted. Nellie would say she'd brought it on herself, but it left a bitter taste in Belinda's mouth.

"Hey, girls. How's it going?" Jeff turned off the ignition and climbed out of the car.

It was not the same car he had been driving, but a plain, black Chevrolet, probably five or six years old.

"Like it?" he asked as both sets of eyes scanned the shiny exterior.

"It's boring," Nellie replied. "I like your other one better."

"It's nice," Belinda said, annoyed with her sister's rudeness.

"Wanna go for a ride?" Jeff asked.

"We've been in cars before," Nellie answered for them before Belinda had a chance to respond. "Besides, Belinda's grounded. I could go, but I'd rather not."

"Oh. Okay." Jeff's smile dipped into a frown. "So what's happenin'?"

"I'm just drying apples with my mudder. Nellie was dusting. Same old stuff. How's school going?" The three of them started walking toward the house, Nellie obviously absorbing every word.

"Good, so far. There's a lot of homework involved. I only got about five hours sleep last night."

"That's not enough. You'll flunk out," Nellie said.

Belinda released a sharp breath, an unspoken word on the tip of her tongue. What a brat her sister had become.

"I can function, but not great," he added, looking over at Nellie.

"I'm glad I don't have to go to college. I just wanna get married and have boppli," Nellie continued. "That's what all Amish women want."

"You can't speak for every single Amish woman, Nell," Belinda said, biting her words as they exited.

"Most. The gut ones anyway. Ain't that what you want, Belinda?"

"I'd rather not discuss it."

"Ladies, no arguing. Good Amish women stay nice and calm."

"Not always. You should hear Belinda sometimes. Goodness, can she yell."

Jeff burst out laughing. "Really? How about that. What do you have to say for yourself, Belinda?"

"Ohhhhh. Nellie, go in the kitchen. I want to take a walk with Jeff."

"Mamm said—"

"I don't care what she said. Just go!"

"I'm telling on you. You're not supposed to be alone with guys, especially.... You know that."

"Jeff's a friend. For Pete's sake, we were together six hours on the trip home from Pennsylvania and Mamm and Daed knew all about it."

"That's different. He was driving. What could you do?"

"Nellie! Stop it!"

Jeff continued to look amused, but he reached over and patted Nellie on the shoulder. "It's okay. We'll skip the walk and the three of us can sit together and play a card game or something."

"I don't like cards."

"What do you like?"

"Quilting."

"Oh, brother," Belinda let out.

"I'm afraid my stitches are too big for that," Jeff said with a grin reaching across his face.

"Guys don't quilt," Nellie said, crossing her arms as they walked. "You're teasing me."

"I don't want to play any games with Nellie," Belinda remarked as they entered the kitchen.

Grace looked up from the apples. "Hallo, Jeff. What brings you here today?" she asked, her face set without a smile.

"Just thought I'd stop by to see how everyone is doing," he said as Belinda pointed to a chair, which he sat upon. "Can I help?"

"Nee, that's all right. I'm tired of doing these apples, though. I'm going to quit for a while. Belinda, do we have any rice pudding left from last night?"

"A little."

"I guess you could have some, if you want, Jeff."

"I think I'll hold off for now."

"I hear you're in school. I bet that keeps you busy." Grace went to the sink to wash her hands. She turned back as she reached for a terry hand towel.

"It does. That's why I haven't been around much. Is Mr. Glick outside? I have a magazine I want to show him."

"He's out there somewhere. He should be taking a break soon, though."

"Mamm, can Jeff stay for dinner?"

"Well, I guess. Hope we have enough meatloaf."

"You made a huge one. Remember?"

"Jah, you're right. Sure, you're welcome to stay." Grace shot a glance over at her daughter.

"Thanks, I'd like that. Let me call home and tell Mom." He reached in his pants pocket and extracted his cell phone. After leaving a message he went out to look for Belinda's father, leaving the three women together in the kitchen.

"Mamm, Nellie is being a brat. You have to do something about it."

"I am not. I only did what you said, Mamm. I stuck with them, real close."

"Jah, closer than honey on a bear. She's driving me crazy. What do you think I'm going to do? Run away or something?"

"Now, now. Nellie, you don't have to be annoying. Keep your mouth closed and just keep them company."

"Is that necessary, Mamm?" Belinda asked. "I mean, really! I'm a big girl now."

Nellie placed her hands on her hips. "Jah and you got in trouble with the police. Real smart." She glared at her sister.

"Don't bring that up again. Mamm, don't let her talk about that. You know how upset it makes me."

"You're right. Nellie, enough now. Why don't you go pick some corn for tonight?"

"But you told me—"

"*Nellie.*" Grace's tone left nothing to wonder about. Nellie grabbed a basket, let out a humph, and slammed the screen door behind her.

Belinda let out a sigh of relief. "She's enough to make me hate kinner."

Grace grinned. "She can be annoying."

"Please don't have her follow me around like this. I'll stay within sight of the house if you'll only let me have my time alone."

"With Jeff?" Grace's eyebrows rose.

"It can be Jeff or Carrie, or anyone, really. I just don't need her company. She's a little monster sometimes."

"All right. I'll talk to her, but I'm going to keep my eye on you, Belinda. You know I don't like the idea of you seeing so much of an Englisher."

"He's a Mennonite now. Didn't you see his new car? It's totally black with no decoration."

"When did that happen?"

"Recently, but he's talked about changing over for a long time now. He's practically Amish."

"But he's *not.* Don't forget that. It would break my heart for you to leave the Amish. What about Zeke? I know for a fact he has his eye on you."

"Mamm, really now. I can find my own boyfriend. Zeke is nice, but he doesn't send off any sparks."

Grace shook her head. "My, my. So now you need sparks to seal a relationship."

"Didn't you have any when you met Daed?"

"Nee. I don't remember any fireworks. I liked him and thought he was cute, but no lightning."

"Well, you know what I mean. You have to have more than a friendship if you're gonna marry someone. After all…"

"Oh, jah, you're right. Now let's get the table set. Your daed will come in starving soon and I want to serve the meatloaf while it's hot."

Belinda set a place for Jeff next to Gideon and placed Nellie's setting as far from hers as she could. Oh, my. She wished she were the youngest in the family. It wasn't easy being older and having to put up with her sibling's shenanigans.

Chapter Eight
Lancaster County, Pennsylvania

Priscilla's mouth dropped open when Katie and Josiah appeared on the staircase together.

No one spoke. Finally Priscilla managed to utter a few words about being in the neighborhood and stopping by to leave off fresh parsley, which was nowhere in sight.

"Uh, danki. I don't cook with...a... parsley, though." Josiah stood, pulling on his suspenders, licking his dry lips. Katie remained mute.

"I didn't see your buggy, Katie. I guess it's in the back. So, anyway, I guess I'd better run. I'm meeting friends for lunch." Priscilla turned to leave.

Katie found her tongue. "How's John?"

"Oh, he's okay, I guess. We're not engaged anymore," she said with a slight stutter.

"Sorry to hear that," Katie responded, meaning it sincerely. The blonde beauty had always had eyes for Josiah.

Katie and Josiah walked down the stairs and Katie stood motionless as Priscilla made her way toward the door and exited.

"See you." Priscilla walked rapidly toward her buggy, without a look back.

Strange, Katie thought to herself as she reached the doorway, she had even taken the harness off the horse and tethered him. After Priscilla finally got started down the drive, Katie turned toward Josiah, who was fidgeting with his straps, ignoring her eyes.

"So, I wonder why she stopped by. She even walked in without knocking."

"Uh, she had extra parsley, I guess."

"Has she stopped before?"

"Well...maybe once, or twice, just for a couple minutes. She's just a friend."

"Mmm. I wonder." Katie couldn't believe the cool voice she heard coming from her own mouth. Inside she was screaming. Inside she was panicking. Yet to hear her, you'd think she was asking about the weather. "Well, maybe I understand why you don't have much time anymore to visit me. Maybe I do."

"Katie, it's not what you think. Really. Okay, once in a while she comes by and we play cards or something. You're my girl, not her."

"She has a pretty bad reputation. Maybe what you see in her is something else. Like a gut time, maybe?"

"Kate, for heaven's sake. That's a terrible thing to say. Priscilla ain't that bad. She's just friendly, is all."

"Oh, yah. She's friendly with all kinds of guys. Real friendly! I'm leaving now. Get my buggy for me."

"Now, Katie, don't go off in a fit. Come on. I'll make you a sandwich. I have bologna. Homemade."

"I don't care if you have roast duckling! I'm going home!"

"Not like this. Come on." He tried to pull her toward him in an embrace, but Katie pushed him away and started toward the back door. "That's okay. I'll get my own buggy. Don't bother to come by for a while. I have too much to do to waste time with a two-timer."

"Katie! Stop it! Just because someone stops by—"

"That someone being a beautiful, loose girl named Priscilla Miller! Sorry, Josiah. I don't believe you. I think you want to have it all. A fiancé, a good reputation, and a disgusting affair!"

"That's enough, Katie! You're way over the line on this. I have to admit, I can't believe you don't trust me. Look, every time I come over to see you, you have an excuse to avoid my kisses. A guy likes to know his girl thinks he's special. I've really been wondering."

"Have you? Wow! How understanding! Here I am taking care of an elderly invalid and you're fooling around cause you can't wait for me to be free. Really nice. Yeah, you're a real great guy! I'm glad I found out the truth about you before it was too late. I'm ending the engagement right now. This very minute! She can have you... you and your crummy house!"

That wasn't nice. That was downright mean. Katie's heart was breaking, but she never meant to be cruel. He'd worked so hard making a home for them. Why did he mess up so? Why was that boy-crazy girl in his, *no—their* home? After climbing into the buggy, nearly tripping over her skirt, Katie snapped the whip in the air and felt the horse bolt off and head out the drive. She didn't look back. She wouldn't have seen anything anyway. Her tears were too plentiful and the black dots were overtaking her sight. *Oh, dear God. Help me.*

Holmes County, Ohio

Supper went well. Sort of. At least Nellie kept her mouth shut for a change. Her mother took her aside to suggest she remain out of sight after the meal was cleaned up. Belinda watched as Nellie twisted her mouth and sneaked a peek at her as she nodded. "All right, but you're taking your chances, Mamm," she added in a stage whisper.

Belinda rolled her eyes. In the meantime the men had headed outside. Belinda watched as her father and Jeff stood outside the barn door leafing through a landscaping magazine— animatedly talking. Her father really liked Jeff. She didn't believe there'd be a problem convincing him to accept her union with a non-Amish man, since he was so close, now that he was becoming a Mennonite.

She wondered if his decision had anything to do with his feelings for her, but she remembered he'd talked about it from the first time they talked. The first time. She couldn't quite remember when that was. It might have been at the market place where their families had their stands. Probably. She remembered thinking how good-looking he was and what gentle eyes he had. She even recalled having a desire for him, but his not being Amish had made a major difference in her thinking back then.

She never had looked upon him as a potential suitor, though she admitted she might have liked having him for a boyfriend. For a little while. And now she was his fiancé. How exciting. And there *were* fireworks and sparkles. It might be a year or two before they'd actually marry. That was a long time, but in the meantime, she'd learn how to cook better and he'd be working toward a career. They'd have enough money to purchase their own place, especially if she could work part-time and save to help out. Maybe she could get a job at night baby-sitting for some rich Englishers. Or sell a quilt or two. She heard about a woman who sold one at auction for a thousand dollars! Of course, that woman was a perfectionist. She had gorgeous quilts and made her own designs. Nee, she'd have to stick to baby-sitting.

"Belinda," her mother's voice came through to her.

"Jah?"

"I asked if you remembered Rachel and Reuben plan to stop over in a while. I made four coconut custard pies earlier. I hope Jeff will be gone by then."

"Why? He doesn't eat that much."

"It's not that. You know why. I think he's smitten with you and I don't want him turning your head."

"Oh, Mamm. My goodness, I'm a big girl now."

"That's what I'm afraid of. You're a very attractive young woman, whether you know it or not, and sometimes the English men try to take advantage of our girls. I've seen it happen more than once. Remember Ada Graber's dochder?"

"Jah, I remember. Poor thing. She had to leave town."

"Jah, and I can name a few more. You watch yourself young lady. They don't respect women the way the Amish men do."

"Jeff isn't like that. He's very respectful."

"Oh, jah? So has he ever tried to kiss you?" Her mother stood back and placed her hands on the sides of her apron as she stared at her daughter.

"Why would he do that?" She was buying for time. Lying didn't come easy.

"Belinda, you ain't answering my question."

"He...he maybe tried."

"See? Did you stop him?"

"Mamm! Why are you asking me that?"

"You know why. So did you?"

"Please, don't get so personal."

"I take that as a yes. Oh, Belinda, you be wary. I'm getting white hair because of you. Why can't you be more like your older sister?"

"Every time. I'm always being compared. Rachel this. Rachel that. Little Miss Perfect. I'm sick of it! Why do you think I rebelled for awhile?"

"Oh, so that was why? Please. I don't want to hear it."

The door swung open and Jed and Jeff walked in. They stopped and took in the scene before them. The women's voices had reached them outside. Belinda prayed the words had been too muffled to distinguish. Goodness, how embarrassing if Jeff heard them arguing about kisses!

"Nellie said you made my favorite pie today, Grace. We came in to get some, but if it's poor timing, we can..."

"Nee. It's fine. Sit. Sit. I hoped Rachel and Reuben would be here by now, but you can have your piece, Jeff. I know you've probably got lots of studying to do."

"Oh, I finished it before—"

"Jah, I guess you'll have to leave soon," Belinda added, trying to catch his eye, but he was studying the pie instead of her. Grace handed him the first piece before he realized what they had said. He looked over at Belinda with raised brows.

Belinda tried her best to look pleasant, but her expression was anything but sweet.

Her anger was with her mother, but Jeff had no idea what had transpired before they entered the kitchen. His mouth drooped and she knew she'd hurt him. She could explain later—some of it anyhow. Not the questions about kissing. That would be way too embarrassing.

After finishing his pie, Jeff rose to leave. "Well, thanks for dinner. It was delicious. My folks want to have you all over some night for a barbeque. I hope we can work things out."

"That's nice," Grace said, her mouth drawn. "Jah, we'll see. Belinda help me please. Nellie can walk Jeff out."

"I can walk myself out, thanks. Uh, you can keep that magazine, Mr. Glick. I copied the article I wanted."

"Danki. Stop in again. We always enjoy your company."

Grace glared at her husband and thumped several plates on the table before cutting the rest of the pie.

Belinda felt as if she were going to cry. What an awful ending to her day. Now she'd have to endure an evening with her perfect sister, which she would have normally enjoyed. But tonight, she didn't want to be with anyone with an ounce of family blood in his or her veins.

Chapter Nine
Lancaster County, Pennsylvania

The ride home gave Katie little time to put her emotions in order. Not wanting to have to give explanations about her swollen eyes and runny nose, she stopped at a clearing before turning the bend near their property. Her horse pulled at the reins, but she held fast and directed him aloud to stop. She rested a wad of already damp tissues on her blurry eyes and allowed her tears to continue until she was totally drained. This was it. The end of her engagement and all hopes of a wonderful marriage with the man of her dreams. Done. Her future looked bleak. Endless days of nursing care. Laundry. Cooking. Cleaning. No loving husband or adorable boppli to fill her days and her heart. And she had brought some of this on herself. Thinking back, she realized how little time she and Josiah had together over the last several months. But was it her fault? Goodness, couldn't he see she was needed by her family? That given enough time things would return to normal?

Priscilla's startled expression blotted out all other images. Certainly, she wouldn't have looked guilty if it was merely a friendly visit. *Parsley.* She didn't even have any in her hand. And it was the tone of her voice that gave it away. So sweet, so beseeching—*"Josiah, where are you?"* Would she have gone upstairs to check for him? The stories she'd heard about Miss Priscilla! Probably all true. She even admitted her engagement was off with John. *Oh, dear God, help me. I'm hurting so, so bad.*

It took more than an hour to calm herself down enough to return home. Four separate buggies passed her during that hour. She knew everyone who went by, but she kept out of sight, ducking as they passed. Thank goodness, no one stopped to check on her. She'd have to tell people eventually about their break-up. Very few people knew about her relationship with Josiah though. Mainly her family, and of course, her very best friend, Becky. Thankfully, she was coming over that very afternoon to spend time with her. Or was it really to see Wayne? Even though Wayne paid little attention to her friend, Becky hadn't given up all hope of his one day caring for her. Belinda hadn't helped matters when she was staying with the family, though in the end, she hadn't really made a play for him—or for Josiah, though Katie thought he'd taken full notice of Belinda. Jah, she was beautiful, but what a troublemaker.

Toward the end of Belinda's stay, they had worked together to care for Oma. Katie had grown closer to her and admitted she enjoyed her company once they got to know each other. But there had never been full trust.

Katie trusted very few girls—at least when it came to Josiah. And now he'd proven her right. Priscilla. Of all people. Never in her wildest dreams would she have believed he'd leave her for Priscilla, or any other girl. Maybe he *didn't* plan to leave her. Maybe he just wanted a little fling before tying the knot. Wasn't that even worse? Would he then end up an adulterer when they married? Could he ever be trusted again?

"Katie, Katie," she said aloud. "You jump to conclusions too quick-like. Slow down." For the next few minutes, she berated herself and then created optimistic outcomes in her mind.

Finally, she pulled back onto the road and made her way to the farmhouse. By this time, she'd be needed. Oma would be ready for her bath. The clothes would be dry and ready to be folded. When Becky stopped by, she would help, but then it would be time to prepare for the next meal. *Lord, help me. Give me a pure heart and fill me with love for others.*

After turning down the drive to the back she waved over to Wayne, who took the reins as she got down from her seat. He mumbled something as she walked slowly, automatically, toward the house. As she opened the door, she heard Oma call out for her. She needed to use the bathroom.

Fill me with love.

She took a deep breath and headed for Oma's room.

Holmes County, Ohio

Jeff had even more incentive to do well in school and work toward his future now that he and Belinda planned to marry. It would be difficult to wait until marriage for some things. Being a guy wasn't always easy when it came to waiting for fulfillment. Especially with such strong impulses and hormones surging through his body, but wait he would. When they married, it would be with a purity that would honor God. Yes, it would be worth the wait and he knew how keenly Belinda wanted to stay virtuous. She was so lovely—not only in her appearance, but her sweet spirit. Yes, she'd been naive and did some things frowned upon by her community, and even by him, but she had learned a lot in these last weeks. They both had. Jeff depended more and more on his relationship with Christ to give him the strength to adhere to his beliefs. He read his Bible whenever he had a free moment, finding comfort and support in God's word.

Carrie interrupted his thoughts as she joined him on the patio. Their parents were out for the evening with friends, and the sky darkened earlier each night as fall approached. Carrie snapped her jean jacket closed and huddled into a wicker armchair. "Hey, what's up, bro?"

"Not much. I thought you were going out tonight."

"I was, but things changed."

"Who's your latest man of the hour?" he asked, grinning.

"You don't wanna know."

"Uh, oh. Confess."

"Dan."

"Get out. You know better than to fool around with him. He'll never be serious about anyone. He's too in love with himself."

"I think he's changed."

"Really? Remarkable."

"Jeff, give him a chance. We've had some long talks since he's been back from his life-guard job, and I think he's calmed down a lot."

"I'll believe it when I see it."

"You won't see it, if you don't want to."

"Look, Carrie, you know he's gone with just about every girl he's met, and once he gets what he wants, he discards them like dirty towels."

"He used to be that way."

"Carrie, don't be a fool. A leopard doesn't change its spots."

"So you don't believe in redemption?"

"I didn't say that, but you need to repent first. I can't see that guy regretting anything. He even tried to take advantage of Belinda."

"He wouldn't have gone that far."

"Oh, right. I can't believe you're this gullible. There're plenty of nice guys out there. Take your time. You just turned eighteen. You're too young to get serious."

"Who said I was serious? I just enjoy going out with him. He's fun. He makes me laugh."

"Hey, all I can do is warn you. I'm not your father."

"Thank goodness. You'd be one mean dude," she said, smiling over at him. "So what about you and Belinda?"

"What about us?"

"Come on, Jeff. It's pretty obvious you guys are in love."

"It's that obvious?"

"Oh, yeah. Your eyes give it away. Have you proposed yet?"

"Carrie, you're too perceptive. Don't tell anyone, but yeah, we're kind of engaged. Nothing official, but we're really in love, big time."

"That's great, Jeff. I'm really happy for you. I just can't believe she's willing to leave the Amish for you, or anyone."

"Since I'm Mennonite now, we're not that far apart."

"Will she be shunned?"

"I don't think so. She hasn't been baptized yet, so she's free to marry whom she pleases. Besides, their bishop is younger than most and more liberal. He even allows cell phones now."

"But not cars?"

"No. I think that will be the last to go. I'm going to have to have a car. Belinda knows that."

"I can't believe you traded in your sweet car for that black thing. It's so boring."

Jeff laughed. "You get used to it."

"I could never get used to dressing the way they do, though. They're so old-fashioned."

"I like the way they dress. You could stand to be more modest yourself, sis."

"Oh, please. Don't be ridiculous."

"Guys can get the wrong idea."

"You sound like you live in Victorian times. I dress the way all my friends dress. There's nothing immoral about it."

I could debate that, but it wouldn't get me anywhere."

Carrie's cell went off and she broke into a grin when she saw her caller's name. "See you, Jeff. It's Dan." She quickly went into the house as she answered it. He could hear her laughing as she made her way up the stairs to the privacy of her room.

Dan was trouble. Jeff prayed for his sister's protection and reached for a textbook to begin studying. There was just so much he could do, and prayer was his best weapon.

Chapter Ten
Lancaster County, Pennsylvania

After Katie helped Oma use the bathroom, she left her sitting by the window in her bedroom for a change of scenery.

When Katie walked back to the kitchen, her mother looked up from chopping vegetables for soup. "Katie, you were gone so long. Where did you go? Oh, never mind, you're here now. Oma needs her bath. She's been complaining that she's too tired, but we missed yesterday, so we can't put it off again.

"I'll start the water. Becky's coming by in a while, so I hope we'll be done by then."

"She'll just have to wait. She'll understand."

"Mmm. I guess."

Mary looked over at her daughter and noted the puffiness around her eyes. "What's the matter, Katie? Have you been crying?"

"I'm fine. I'll get towels from the line in the basement. We should have hung them out since it didn't make wet after all."

"We had no way of knowing. It sure looked like rain. I brought up some towels before. In fact, I set one aside for Oma. You sure you're okay? Did you go see anyone?"

"Mamm, I don't want to talk about it, okay?"

"Don't be huffy."

"I'm sorry, it's just that... I'll go start her bath."

Mary went into her mother's room to prepare Oma. Mary still had a persistent cough. Oma looked up at her as she began to remove her clothing. "You should go see the doctor, Mary. I don't like the sound of that cough. It wasn't that long ago you had bronchitis."

"I'm not as sick this time. It's probably just the tag end of my illness."

"Still, you're lookin' thin. Pale, too."

"Mamm, don't worry about me. Let me slip your bathrobe over you."

"Where are the men-folk? I don't want them seeing me in my robe."

"Goodness, they've seen you before. Not to worry, Mamm. They're where they always are—outside working."

"Where's Katie? She should be helping."

"She is helping. She's preparing your bathwater."

"I think you could get me upstairs. I don't like that old metal tub you set up in the kitchen. It ain't safe. Anyone could walk in."

"We always put a sign on the door when we bathe you, you know that. No one will come in unless we unlock the door. Now don't talk about climbing that staircase again. We don't need another fall."

"Ach. I hate being such a burden. It would be better if—"

"Now don't start talkin' like that. You're no burden."

"But poor Katie. She was supposed to get married soon."

"She still can. They can stay in the dawdi haus till you're better."

"Oh, Mary, do you think I'll ever really be better?" Her eyes filled and Mary reached over and put her arms around her mother's shoulders.

"Of course. In God's time. You're strong."

"Not anymore. I don't even have the will to try. I'm sorry, honey." She began to weep.

Katie came in the room and looked at them as they held each other. "Oh, my, what's wrong, Oma?"

"I'm okay," she said through her tears. "Come on, let's get this old body washed up so I can take my nap."

The clothes were folded and put away; Oma was bathed and back in her bed for her nap, and preparations were completed for supper. Katie should have felt elated, but her heart was broken.

She heard a buggy on the gravel drive. Maybe, just maybe, it was Josiah coming to proclaim his everlasting love for her. He was probably as grief-stricken as she was.

But no, it was Becky. At least she'd have someone to talk to. She excused herself and walked out to greet her friend, who was parking the buggy next to the barn. Wayne came out and nodded to them. "I'll take care of your horse, Beck. Go talk to Katie."

"Danki. You busy, Wayne?"

"Well, yeah," he said with a smile. "Ain't I always?"

"I guess." Becky's cheeks flushed. "It was a dumb question."

"Nee. Well, maybe a little." He laughed and took hold of the reins.

Becky climbed down and she and Katie walked toward the farmhouse. Once out of Wayne's hearing, Becky whispered, "I feel like such a fool. Why did I ask such a silly question?"

"It doesn't matter? We all say stupid things sometimes. Let's go to my room. I need to talk." Her voice cracked as she ended the sentence and she felt Becky's eyes on her.

"Katie, you look awful. Are you sick?"

"Heartbroken. But we can't talk in front of my mudder. Wait till we get upstairs."

After greetings and an invitation to stay for supper, the girls went up to Katie's room. They sat next to each other on the bed and Becky patted Katie's hand. "Tell me everything."

She did and Becky's eyes widened at the name of Priscilla. She clucked her tongue as Katie gave her a moment-by-moment account of her experience. When she finished, Becky sat back and folded her arms. She had a scowl on her face.

"Maybe it's not what you think. I know Priscilla. She'd think nothing of taking another girl's boyfriend, but Josiah? He's crazy about you. Surely, he wouldn't fall for that...that woman!"

"She's beautiful."

"So? You're just as pretty. Besides, it's not the outer person that counts."

"She's smart and she knows how to make guys laugh."

"You're smart. I don't know about the laughing part."

"Sometimes Josiah laughs at me."

"See? So why would he leave you for her?"

"Maybe he's fed up with me never having time for him. Any guy would get upset after awhile, don't you think?"

"You're in a tough place right now, Katie. He knows it's temporary. Your Oma's getting better, ain't she?"

Katie let out a long weary breath. "I think she's going backwards. She's shakier now than ever and she wants to sleep all the time. It's like she doesn't even want to get better."

"Oh, that's bad. Poor lady. Losing her husband like that and now breaking a hip. I can't say I blame her for not trying real hard."

Katie nodded. "I know, but she'll never get better this way. Oh, Becky, I've lost him. I know it. If he really, really cared, he would have followed me home and begged me to keep our engagement."

"He was probably stunned at everything that happened."

"He sure was *stunned* when little Miss Pris showed up! You should have seen his face."

Becky placed her hand over her mouth, but her eyes crinkled from silent laughter. "I wish I could have seen him. Look, Katie. I really think you'll get back together, but give him some time. Let him miss you some more before you talk to him again. I...I guess I need to tell you something."

Katie looked over, questioning with her eyes? "What?"

"I wasn't going to say anything, but..."

"Tell me!"

"Well, last week I went to the Sing. I was hoping Wayne would be there, but as you know, he wasn't."

"Jah. So?"

"Josiah was there."

"Alone?"

"Kind of."

"What does that mean?"

"He came in alone, but..."

"But?"

"I don't know exactly, but he and Pris were missing for awhile at the same time. Now maybe it didn't mean a thing. You can't jump to conclusions."

"Oh, Becky! How could he? Why did he even go, knowing I wouldn't be there? And why didn't he tell me or come by? Oh, golly, this is getting worse by the minute. It's over. Definitely over. I'm just glad I found out what a horrible person he was before it was too late! I never want to see him again—ever! I may have to move to Ohio, or Philadelphia. I'll live with Aunt Esther! Or maybe I'll leave the Amish and move to Canada!"

"Katie! Stop! We're probably all wrong about Josiah. Let's wait and see how things go. I'll check around and talk to our friends. Maybe they'll know something we don't."

"I don't care anymore. I don't think I even love him anymore. He has no feelings. Poor Oma and Mamm. She's getting sick again, I'm afraid, and I feel horrible myself."

Katie laid her head on Becky's shoulder and cried for several minutes. Becky surrounded her with her arms and rocked her like a child. "Poor Katie. I'm so sorry. If love is like this, I don't want to ever fall in love."

"It shouldn't be. Mercy, look at my brudders and Daed. They're great husbands. I should have known Josiah was fickle the way he ran after my schwesters, Ruthie and Emma. He's just girl crazy, is all."

"He's immature, to say the least. He'll be sorry someday, Katie, real sorry."

Katie nodded through her tears. "I hope you're right. I'm not going to waste any more tears on him or any other guy. I know God is in control of my life, Becky, and maybe he has someone a hundred times nicer for me down the road. But for now, I'm needed here and I'm going to help as much as I can."

"Katie, you're such a gut person. I'm honored to be your friend. Josiah can jump in the lake. Oh, and Wayne with him.'"

Katie smiled through her tears. "Or the pond. It's closer."

Chapter Eleven
Holmes County, Ohio

Carrie lay on her bed as she tucked her cell phone under her ear. Dan's voice murmured softly and she pictured the handsome young man as she had seen him the night before. Clean-cut, dazzling blue eyes, and immaculate clothes. Even in old worn jeans, he walked with an air of confidence. He was headed somewhere and he knew it and so did everyone he met. Yes, he liked women, but what guy didn't? Her brother worried too much about her. She could handle Dan. He wasn't the first guy she'd ever dated. She had to tamper down another guy's amour once. Dan was no different.

"So what do you think?" he was asking her something and she'd been sidetracked, thinking about him.

"Sorry?"

"About going out tomorrow night. I heard there's a group playing live at the club around dinnertime. Then they'll have dancing. You can get dressed up like you said you wanted to."

"Really? A real honest-to-goodness dress?" She laughed into the phone.

"I'd like that. I'll pick you up at seven and we'll eat there. My treat."

"Sure. It's a Saturday night, so I guess I can stay out late."

"I have to get back to college Sunday morning. A friend is having a brunch for her engagement and I promised I'd be there, so I can't stay out all night."

"Dan, I didn't expect you to. I'll have to be home by one anyway."

"Oh, yeah, I forgot. You go off to college this week, right?"

"I told you I did. You never listen. We're leaving Thursday. I met my dorm mate on Skype. She seems real nice."

"That's good. Listen, I have to run. See you tomorrow night. Wear something sexy."

Carrie giggled. "Dan, you're so bad. I'll wear whatever I want."

His laugh came over the phone. "You always look sexy, no matter what you wear, so don't worry about it."

"Believe me, I won't," she said, grinning. "See you then."

She lay there after they hung up and pictured the dresses in her closet. She had a red silk with a deep v-neck, which would show the most cleavage, but her father hadn't seen it yet and he'd probably throw a fit. Maybe she could wear a jacket over it so he wouldn't notice. Then she had a navy cotton, not as dressy, but classy. Definitely not sexy. She rose and went over to her closet and pushed the few dresses she owned along, examining each one through Dan's eyes.

A white rayon dress with cap sleeves and a flowing skirt attracted her eyes. She'd only worn it once, but it had attracted a lot of attention from the guys. Dan hadn't seen it yet. She tried it on and looked in her full-length mirror. It was perfect. It fit snuggly on top, accentuating her full bust line and yet made her waist look smaller than it was. Definitely sexy, and yet not cheap the way some girls dressed. Dan would be pleased. Her parents? Maybe not so much, but her mother had been with her when she picked it out, so it couldn't be too bad. Her father was just old-fashioned. And Jeff? Even worse. He was way too protective of her. Hopefully, now that he had Belinda in his life, he'd leave her alone. She told him she was going to remain pure and she had no intention of changing her mind. None whatsoever.

Jeff closed his textbook and looked out across the pool It was the last week in August and the sun was setting. Streaks of color reached across the horizon, vying for attention. It was quite a show as the colors deepened, visible above the tall grasses planted along the fringe of the pool area. He was proud of the way his landscaping ideas had formulated. Even his boss wanted pictures to show potential customers. A Japanese maple rested in a corner and draped gracefully over the artificial boulders placed artistically underneath. A few dwarf evergreens were tucked along the side with dazzling colors of annual flowers between them, massed by color.

Jeff wondered what Belinda was doing at this very moment. Probably cleaning up from supper. She was constantly active, always busy with something. If she sat after a meal, she'd either mend or work on a quilt with her sister, Nellie. What a nice family. How fortunate he was to have a wonderful girl like Belinda in love with him, willing to spend the rest of her life with him. Her parents would have to be told soon, so they wouldn't feel they were being betrayed. That was the last thing he wanted. He had a good relationship with Belinda's father, which he didn't want to change. If only her mother was more receptive. In time.

Maybe he should go see Belinda this evening. He had finished his schoolwork and it was Friday night. Even though her parents owned a cell phone now, they frowned on it being used for anything besides an emergency. Of course, it was kind of an crisis, he told himself with a smile. After all, he was almost sick not being with her. Wasn't that sort of an emergency?

Carrie came through the patio door and sat down beside him. "Nice evening."

"It is. Cool." They watched as the lightning bugs began their dance through the grasses, dots of shining mica in the sky. "We're lucky to grow up in such a beautiful location."

"Yeah. Nice to have money, too," Carrie said as she stretched her tanned legs and rested them on a low metal table.

"Are you excited about starting college?"

"Excited, and a little scared."

"Really? You?"

"Why not me? I mean, this is going to be a totally new experience. On my own and all. No one around to tell me what to do. I think I'll like it, a lot. How come you didn't want to go away to school, Jeff?"

"It's cheaper to stay home."

"But you weren't going to pay for it."

"Still. Besides, this way I can see my friends more often."

"Like Belinda?" She gave a crooked smile and tossed her hair back.

He grinned back. "Maybe."

"So when are you going to talk to her parents?"

"We have to wait awhile. She's still on probation." He took a sip of iced tea and moved back on the chaise.

"She hardly did anything. They're way too strict." Carrie swatted a mosquito, which landed on her leg.

"She snuck out at night to be with her friends and then in Pennsylvania, she attended a party where there were drugs."

"But she didn't know it, did she?"

"Still, she didn't use her head."

"Jeff, you sound more like a father or big brother than her future husband."

"I can be both. I do feel like protecting her."

"Just like you feel responsible for your little sister?"

He shook his head. "Got me there. Okay, so maybe I carry it too far, but I can't help it. I know you and Belinda. You're both really good people, but I'm afraid you're also gullible."

"I'm not. I'm fully aware of the dangers in dating a guy like Dan, but I know I can handle him."

"Right. He's pretty persuasive. I know a couple girls who thought they could handle him…"

"Well, trust me on this. We're going out tomorrow night. Dinner and dancing."

"Oh, great. I give up trying to talk sense into you. You're on your own."

"Gee, thanks, bro. I love your trust in me."

"I trust you, just not Mr. Romeo." He wrapped his arms around his muscular legs and shook his head.

"I'll give you a full account of our evening on Sunday."

"Are you going to church with me?"

"Depends on what time we get home."

"Late service is at eleven."

"I'll see. Don't push me, Jeff. Really, I don't like that."

"Sorry, you're right. Okay, if you're up in time and want to go, just let me know. Last word on the subject."

She reached across and patted his arm. "Thanks. You're a pretty neat brother. God was good when he put me in this family."

He released his hold on his legs and covered her hand with one of his. "Just be careful. I kinda like my sister, too."

She nodded and they sat silently as they watched the stars become visible against the blackening sky.

Lancaster County, Pennsylvania

After Becky left, Katie and her mother helped Oma prepare for bed. First they walked her to the bathroom where she brushed her teeth and took care of her other needs. Katie stood by watching the elderly woman as she brushed with one hand and held on to the side of the sink with her other. Her arm trembled slightly. It was sad to watch her deteriorating before her very eyes. She realized what a privilege it was to be able to serve her family in this small way. If it meant losing Josiah because of his selfishness, so be it. Some things were more important.

Katie glanced over at her mother who was folding and neatening the towels on the racks. She began coughing and covered her mouth as her upper body shook. Tomorrow she'd insist on her mother going to the doctor. Her father, Leroy, mentioned it at supper and said he wasn't going to take no for an answer. Concern was written on his face. Her mother finally agreed. Katie knew if he hadn't insisted, she would have put it off indefinitely.

Katie noticed her own fatigue seemed to be increasing. Ruthie had mentioned it a couple days before when she came by to lend a hand. She wasn't able to stay long, though, since Nathanael was cutting teeth and none too happy. His crying upset Oma to the point where Ruthie left early. She looked fatigued as well with her advancing pregnancy.

Emma had her hands full with the new twins and her other two children. The men were all busy harvesting their crops and making hay for the winter. This was not the time to be thinking of herself. A pity party would have to wait. Too many problems right now. Maybe it was a blessing in disguise. She had little time to dwell on Josiah, though there was a deep sadness, which prevailed throughout her spirit. One that wouldn't leave.

Chapter Twelve
Holmes County, Ohio

Carrie applied mascara and smoothed it in with her fingertips. She wrapped her blonde hair into a chignon and added a rhinestone barrette. The white dress was soft against her body and she glanced in her mirror to check out her total appearance. Satisfied, she reached for an aquamarine silk scarf and positioned it around her shoulders to deflect her parents' eyes from her form-fitting bodice. Her father would not approve.

She could hear Dan's voice from downstairs and recognized her brother's as well. Hopefully, he wouldn't be rude to her date, though their mutual dislike was obvious to all their friends.

After grabbing a small white satin purse, she headed downstairs. Jeff and Dan were standing in the hallway and looked up as she descended.

"Nice." Dan's eyes scanned her as she reached the floor level and he smiled broadly.

"Thanks. Shall we go?"

"Have a key, Carrie? We're all gonna be out tonight."

"I always carry an extra key, so have fun with Belinda. I gather that's whom you're going to be with," she added as she and Dan headed toward the door.

Dan turned and laughed. "What, that little Amish girl?"

"Little? She's pretty normal size, don't you think?" Jeff asked with a bite in his tone.

"I guess you're more her type, friend. You can pretend it's 1890."

"Funny."

"Yeah, I thought so. See you later."

Jeff watched as they walked over to Dan's green Porsche and climbed in. Dan didn't even have the courtesy to open the door for his sister. What was she getting into? He shook his head and went up to change his clothes. He hoped Belinda's parents would be all right with his appearing unannounced. It would be a relief when they learned of their relationship. He felt somehow he was being deceptive; acting like his interest was strictly platonic. But, for now, it was necessary.

Dan drove down the drive and took a quick look at Carrie before entering traffic. "You look great. The other guys will have to eat their hearts out."

Carrie laughed. "Glad you like my dress." She allowed the shawl to slip away from her shoulders and he took a double look. "Wow! You're gorgeous."

"You say that to all your dates."

"True, but this time I mean it." He laughed and settled back further in his seat. "A bunch of guys from school are going to be there tonight. I told them about you."

"Oh? What did you tell them?"

"Just that I was coming with a knock-out, and they'd better not try to cut in."

"And if they do?"

"It will be at their own risk."

She felt her heart speed up. He really thought she was that good looking? That's a lot for him, since he only dated the 'in' crowd. Most of the time, anyway. She could think of a couple exceptions—Belinda being one of them. Of course, they didn't actually date, but it was obvious he'd been attracted to her. A twinge of jealousy passed through her. "What about Belinda? Why did you talk about her that way?"

"What way?" He grinned, but kept his eyes on the road. "You mean, like she was insignificant?"

"Yeah. You didn't mean that, did you?"

"I just like to get under your brother's skin. He's so defensive."

"I wish you wouldn't. He's really a great guy. You just have to get to know him better."

"I guess. I'll behave better next time."

"You didn't get very far with Belinda, did you?" She watched his expression, which didn't change one iota.

"As far as I wanted. Why the third degree?"

"Sorry, I just wondered. She is pretty."

"Honey, she doesn't compare to you. You could go to Hollywood, I swear."

It would be easy to be proud with his many compliments, but she reminded herself about his reputation, and took it all in stride. Or tried to.

"So here we are. I'll let the valet park it." He pulled up to the curb and motioned for her to get out her side as he handed keys over to the waiting employee. Then he took her elbow and steered her into the large dining room. Four other couples were sitting at a table for ten and motioned him over.

"I didn't know we were going to be eating with other couples," Carrie said, disappointed.

"I guess I forgot to mention it. You'll like them. I met them in college." He introduced her to everyone and they sat down and picked up their menus. The prices were exorbitant and Carrie was glad they weren't going Dutch.

After ordering, the topic of conversation turned toward college courses and she sat back and observed his friends. They all looked older than Dan, but well heeled, as her father called the rich. Later, while they had dessert and coffee, a five-piece band began to play dance music. One of the guys took his partner on the dance floor and Dan held out his hand. "Ready to dance?"

"Always ready. I love to dance. You know that."

They showed off a few steps and then he steered her toward a dark section of the dance floor, drawing her closer. Uncomfortably close. She didn't like the feelings, which arose by his nearness. Even his after-shave was enticing. Carrie pulled back.

"What's wrong?"

"Nothing. Just that I follow better if I have a little space."

"Oh, sorry. Your eyes look like stars tonight." His voice had lowered half an octave and she glanced up at him. He was very handsome and she didn't want to seem like a prude, but his line sounded artificial.

"Dan, you don't have to say things like that to me. I'm having a good time without you making stuff up to say."

"I mean it. They shimmer—just like your hair. I want to be close to you. Real close."

This was not expected. He was moving way too quickly.

"You're about as close as you're going to get," she said, trying to sound humorous and yet serious at the same time. He looked annoyed.

"Sure. That's fine." He moved back another foot and firmly guided her around the dance floor. He didn't even try to converse any more with her, instead engaging his friends in conversation after they returned to their table.

Carrie was taken by surprise when he suggested she dance with one of the other guys and he reached his hand over to the man's date seated next to him, and asked if she wanted to be his partner for the next set. The girl beamed and stood right up, leaving Carrie with a near stranger. As Paul, her new dance partner, steered her across the floor, she glanced over at Dan, who was entertaining his new dance partner with his vibrant personality. What nerve!

Paul asked her about her plans for college and they talked about the weather and non-essentials. When the two couples returned to their table, Carrie noticed Dan slip a piece of paper in his pocket and wink at the girl.

Around half past twelve, Dan suggested they return home. He was quiet all the way back to her house. She hadn't meant to offend him by suggesting he was working too quickly, but she was concerned about his reputation. Perhaps it was all true. Maybe he was out for what he could get. She was not that kind of girl and if this was the end of their dating, then so be it.

He walked her up to the front door and she took out her key and turned the lock. "Thanks, Dan. It was a nice evening."

"It could get nicer. Can I come in?"

"No one's home, it wouldn't be—"

"Come on, Carrie. I'm not going to try anything. I just feel bad we're ending the evening on a sour note. I promise I'll behave."

"Well, just for a couple minutes." She walked in first and they seated themselves in the living room on the large white damask sofa. She moved as far into the corner as she could and he grinned.

"Scared?"

"Of course not!"

Laughing, he reached for her hand. She allowed him to hold it briefly.

"I don't bite, honest."

"We're close enough. It's only our first real date," she added.

"Then we'll have a second date?"

She blushed. "It depends, I guess."

"On?"

"Well, are you going to ask me?"

"Of course. Right now. Will you go to a movie with me next week-end?"

"I'm planning to stay at school until the end of October. Maybe then."

"It's a date. I'll call you at school to remind you."

She felt safer. It would be a month before they saw each other again. He would have cooled off by then. He was fun to be with and she felt confident she'd put him in his place. A half hour later, he left, without even attempting to kiss her goodnight. Jeff would be pleased to hear about his good manners. Yes, he'd be pleased—even more so than she was. "He could have tried, anyway," she said aloud, as she prepared for bed.

Lancaster County, Pennsylvania

Ruthie came by early to stay with Oma while Leroy took Mary to the doctor's. Katie decided to go along, since the medical building was next door to the grocery store and she needed to purchase more coffee.

"Katie, come in with us," her mother said as Leroy helped her climb out of the buggy.

"Sure. I only have one item to buy. Shouldn't take long after you're done with your appointment."

They walked into the waiting room and as usual, heads turned toward them as they waited to check in. Katie should have been used to it, but it still bothered her.

"The doctor will be with you in just a few moments," the pleasant round-faced nurse said.

Leroy nodded and they sat down near each other. Katie picked up an old magazine and leafed through it. My, the styles girls wore now are so ugly. She skipped to the food section. Maybe she should mention the night sweats to the doctor when he was done examining her mother. Nee, it was probably all the stress she was under. Caused anxiety. Even the fatigue could be explained away. Once Oma was on her own more, then things would become normal. Normal? What was normal anymore? Once she knew exactly what her future would hold, but no longer. It looked bleak. Very bleak.

They were called in to the examination room ten minutes later. After preliminary checks and reviewing Mary's chart, the doctor asked her to sit on the examination table while he listened to her chest and heart. He was very thorough as he worked silently. Then he moved over to his desk and began entering notations into the computer.

"Am I okay?" Mary asked as she shifted her prayer kapp on her head and straightened her apron.

"Your bronchitis has returned, Mary. We need to get you on antibiotics again. This time you'll need to be off your feet until your chest is thoroughly clear. Can you do that?"

"But my mudder—mother. She needs a lot of care."

"I can handle it, Mamm," Katie said.

The doctor looked over his glasses at her. "Katie, you're showing signs of fatigue yourself. Have you been ill?"

"Nee. I'm fine, just tired out, is all."

The doctor turned to Leroy. "Is there someone else in the family who can look after your mother-in-law so we can get these two gals back to normal?"

"I don't know." Leroy's brows drew together. "My dochders are all busy with their young families. They try to help out, but it's hard."

"I can look into a good nursing home if—"

"Nee, my mother's not going into a nursing home." Mary folded her arms and scowled. "We take care of our own."

Leroy spoke up, "Honey, maybe just for a couple weeks. Look at Katie. She's exhausted."

Mary and the doctor turned to Katie. "When I'm done here, I'd like to examine you, Katie. You're very pale."

"I don't get in the sun much."

"Still, if it's okay with your parents?"

Leroy nodded. "Gut idea. I've been concerned, too."

After he wrote the prescription for Mary, Katie's parents left the room to allow more privacy and the doctor took Katie's blood pressure, temperature and pulse. Then he listened to her heart and lungs.

"I have something weird happen sometimes at night. I get these awful hot spells and my sheets get wet from perspiration. It's been happening more frequently lately. They are really annoying."

"Mmm. Shortness of breath?"

"Sometimes."

"Fatigue?"

"Oh, jah, but I do a lot of work."

"I'm sure you do, Katie. It's probably nothing, but I'm going to send you to the lab for blood work. We don't want to miss anything. Do you have time today?"

"I guess so."

"Good." He called his nurse and asked for Katie's chart and then made some notes. He wrote the order for the blood work and walked her out to her parents who were seated in the waiting room. "We're just going to do a blood work-up. It shouldn't be long."

"Mercy, is she sick?" Mary asked.

"We just want to make sure everything is okay. She's thinner than I like to see." He turned toward Katie. "I'd like to have you back again in three days. Make an appointment. And Mary, I'll have you return in two weeks. Now if you can't get help with your mother, you'll have to let me know so I can make other arrangements. Your lungs are weakened and it's going to be harder to keep you well if we don't correct this now. Understand?"

"Oh, jah. I suppose so. I'll find someone to help out."

After the blood was drawn, they went back to their buggy. Leroy seated the two women and went to purchase the coffee. At first, Katie was going to insist on going with him, but she really was drained, so she accepted his offer and sat in the back seat of the buggy.

"Mamm, who can you get to help? Everyone has little boppli or is expecting. Aunt Esther is teaching again."

"I'm not sure, but I'm wondering if Belinda would be willing to return, just for a couple weeks until we get our strength back."

Belinda. Goodness, was she their only option? Would she be willing? Katie said a prayer as her father climbed in with the coffee and clucked for the horse to return home. If it was God's will, then it would be done. She might be gut company at that.

Chapter Thirteen
Holmes County, Ohio

As Jeff drove around to the back of Belinda's home, he spotted her father and Gideon as they came out of the barn. They waved to him when he rolled down his window. "Hi, I thought I'd stop by to see how things are going here."

"Pretty gut," Jed answered as he nodded. "Came at a perfect time. Our Belinda made fresh lemon sponge pies. Three of them. Go park your car and come in the back."

When Jed and Gideon came in the kitchen door, Belinda was nowhere in sight. "Where's our wayward dochder?" Jed asked Grace as she wiped off the counters from supper.

"In the basement. She's looking for pickles we made last year. I want to finish them up before we start on the new ones."

"Can she see gut enough down there? It's getting dark out, and besides, we have company."

"Oh, jah? Who may I ask?"

"Young Jeff. I told him about the pie. Put some extra *kaffi* on, Grace. I'll call Belinda."

"I'm here," she said as she heard her name called. She closed the basement door behind her. "I couldn't find any more pickles, Mamm. I think we already used them up."

With that, Jeff opened the back door and let himself in.

"Goodness, you shocked me," Belinda said, grasping her kapp ribbons in her hand.

"Sorry," Jeff said, grinning widely. "I hear you have lemon sponge pie waiting to be eaten."

"Oh, jah, it's crying out for some hungry men," she said, smiling back.

Grace's stone expression was not lost on her family. Nellie looked over and frowned in her mother's direction. "I'll get the plates and forks."

"Can I help?" Jeff asked.

"Nee, we have it all together," Grace said, not changing her expression, which bordered on rude.

Jed took note and appeared to overcompensate by being extra friendly. "I read that magazine you left from cover to cover. Lots of gut articles in there."

"It's a good magazine. I should be getting the next issue soon. I'll bring it by."

"Jah, that's nice of you. How's school going?" Jed asked.

"Pretty good. I get a lot of homework, but if I put my mind to it, I can get through it pretty quickly."

"Jah, you're smart," Belinda said as she cut the pie and slid a large piece on a plate for their guest.

Jeff smiled over as Nellie passed out the forks.

"Kaffi will be a minute," Belinda added with a sweet smile.

"Thanks, Nellie," Jeff said as he accepted a fork. "Did you help bake them?"

"Not this time, but I know how."

"Belinda made them," Jed said.

"And her mudder," Grace added, looking over at her husband.

"Oh, jah, that's right. I forgot."

Once the pie was eaten, Jeff rose, stacked the soiled dishes and took them over to the sink.

"You don't have to do that," Grace said, running the water over them. "That's women's work."

"I don't mind."

"Better leave it for us. I don't want broken plates," she added without a smile.

"Mamm, that's not nice," Belinda said, unable to keep the shock out of her voice. "He was just being polite."

"Never you mind. Go sit down. I got it."

"I'll help, Mamm," Nellie said, reaching for the dishcloth.

"So let's go sit down," Jed said, motioning for them to go into the living room. Belinda sat across from Jeff and her father, who had taken opposite ends on the sofa. For a moment it was silent and then Jeff and Jed began a discussion about the crops. It had been an excellent year and the Amish families were grateful to God for the plentiful harvest.

Belinda watched as her father and the man she hoped to one day marry bonded. There would be no objection from her daed, that was for certain. Her mamm? That was another matter. Belinda was glad she hadn't taken her kneeling vows already, though she had contemplated doing so at the start of the summer. This way she believed she could keep her relationship with her family, practice the Mennonite religion, and marry the man of her dreams.

The ring of the cell phone, which sat on the mantle, interrupted their discussion. It never rang, unless it was an emergency. Jed's smile turned down as he reached for the phone. Belinda and Jeff exchanged looks. Hopefully, it was good news. By the look on her father's face, it was the opposite. Mercy, Lord have mercy. What could it be?

The conversation was brief and ended with Jed saying he'd discuss something with the family and get back to the person that very day. When he hung up, he looked over at Belinda. "You're needed back in Pennsylvania."

Her heart dropped. Not now. She finally was home and happily engaged to the man of her dreams. Surely they could manage without her. "Why do they want me back?" Her voice cracked and she glanced over at Jeff, whose mouth was taut.

"Seems Oma's dochder, Mary, is sick again and Katie is worn down from exhaustion."

"But they have a ton of relatives. Surely someone else could help out."

"All I know is they asked for our help. Maybe there ain't anyone else available. Leroy said it would probably only be for a couple weeks until his wife is better. I don't know what to say, Belinda. It should be your decision."

"Well, I don't want to go."

"And you think that's the right thing to do?" His brows met and his lips turned down.

"I...I don't know if it's right, but I really just got home and I want to stay here now."

"Let's talk to your mamm about it." Jed stepped over the threshold to the kitchen and motioned for Grace to join them. She wiped her hands and followed him back into the living room.

"Jah? What's wrong?"

"Didn't you hear the phone ring?"

"Jah, so who was it?"

"Leroy Zook. Seems they need Belinda's help again. Everyone's either sick or unable to help with the old lady's care."

"Belinda just got home. Surely, there's someone else they could get with that large family."

"I'm just telling you what they asked. She don't have to go."

Her mother turned toward Belinda. "What do you want?"

"I don't want to leave again. It's not like I wouldn't like to help out, but..."

"What will they do if she doesn't go?" Grace looked back at her husband.

"I guess they'd look for a nursing home for a few weeks."

"Ach. That ain't right." Grace turned back to her daughter. "You should go, Belinda. It's the Christian thing to do."

"But, Mamm—"

"Think about it, Belinda. If it was reversed and we needed help, don't you think they'd come to us?"

"I don't know." Belinda knew she was losing the argument quickly. She should be gracious about it. But leaving Jeff? She looked over and he was leaning over, arms on knees, head down. There was nothing he could say—or would say. He had no stake in this. Then he looked up. "I could drive you there if you want," he said, softly.

Jed nodded. "Jah, you're a gut man, Jeff. They want her to come as soon as possible."

Belinda felt tears forming, but she swallowed several times and stood erectly. "All right, if everyone thinks I should go, then I will. If it's only a couple weeks, I guess I can manage."

Grace nodded. "You'd better do a wash. You have to take clean clothes."

"Do you want to plan to leave Sunday?" Jeff asked. "I'm afraid I need to work tomorrow and it's too late to cancel."

"Sunday's fine. It's visiting Sunday anyway. So I'll just visit my family in Pennsylvania, is all." She attempted to smile, but it took every effort. At least she and Jeff would have all day Sunday together. And maybe she'd be back in two weeks or even sooner. Surely Katie was strong enough to manage alone if need be. She probably just needed some rest. In her heart, she knew it was the right thing to do. The Amish way. God's way. And even if she became a Mennonite, she'd try to live as she'd been raised. Her heart would always be Amish.

Chapter Fourteen
Lancaster County, Pennsylvania

The knock on the front door was persistent. Family and friends always came in the back by the kitchen, so Katie was surprised to find her doctor standing at the door when she answered it.

"Katie, I didn't have a record of you owning a phone and I had to ride right past your place, so...can I come in?"

"Jah. Sorry, please come in. I was just surprised to see you here."

He asked if her parents were available to speak with him also and she explained her mother was still in bed, per his instructions, and her father was outside in the barn. She went and rang the bell to alert them to company, and returned to the hallway. "Please sit down. Daed should be right in. I was just helping my grandmother with her physical therapy."

"Do you need to attend to her now?" He asked.

"Nee, I just got her back in bed."

They discussed the cool weather they were having and mentioned some of the trees turning color. Finally Leroy walked in and the doctor stood long enough to shake hands. Then both men sat down.

"I wanted to stop by and talk to you in person." He cleared his throat. "I'm afraid we got the blood test results back on Katie and well, we need to run more tests. Her levels of red cells and platelets was lower than normal and her white cell count was dangerously high."

"What does that mean?" Leroy sat straight in the chair and locked eyes with the doctor.

"It points to a serious condition. She may have a type of leukemia. I'd like to send her to an oncologist—that's a doctor who specializes in cancer—to run a bone marrow test. It's more conclusive."

Leroy's mouth froze. He finally uttered the dreaded word. "Cancer?"

"Leukemia is now treatable in many cases. People can live normal lives once it's controlled."

Katie stared at his mouth. The words coming out held no meaning. After all, she was young. No one had cancer at her age. It was a bad dream and she'd soon wake up and go about her business.

"Katie?"

She looked at the doctor.

"Do you understand what I just said? We're going to find treatment for you as soon as possible. They have oral drugs now as well as the standard treatments you've heard about."

"What if you can't control it? What if it's too late?" Her voice trembled and she felt as if she was going to black out. Then she felt her father's arms around her and she leaned into him. Her father. Strong, loving. Always there to take away the pain. He'd make her better.

"I'd like you to come into the medical center Monday and we can do the marrow test in the office. I've already spoken to Dr. Humphrey, the oncologist. He's setting aside the time as we speak. Can you bring her in around nine?" he asked Leroy.

He nodded. "We'll be there."

"I'll be able to explain more after we do further testing. I'm sorry to be the bearer of bad news. Hopefully, we've caught it early enough to get it under control quickly." He began walking slowly to the front door. Katie remained seated, but Leroy walked behind him.

"How's Mary today?" the doctor asked, as he reached for the doorknob.

"Not so gut. She coughed most of the night."

The doctor nodded. "It takes a few days before the antibiotics kick in. I'd keep her away from Katie. She doesn't need any further complications right now. Also, you need to find alternative care for your mother-in-law. Katie will need rest while going through her procedures. She's in a weakened state from her illness and then with all this..."

"Jah. It's too much, for sure. Because of Mary and all, I've just made arrangements for a relative to come in from Ohio to help out. Nice girl. She's helped us before. She's coming in Sunday."

"Good. In the meantime, get someone else to help you. I'm surprised Katie's been able to do as much as she has. Leukemia is a terrible drain on the body."

"Jah, my sohn and I can help till Belinda gets here. Maybe I can get one of my other daughters to stay at least part of the time."

The doctor placed his arm on Leroy's shoulder. "We'll do everything we can to make your daughter better, Leroy. You must stay strong."

Leroy nodded, lowering his head to his chest, his beard grazing his work shirt. He blinked his eyes several times and let out a sigh. "God is in charge. We'll accept his will to be done."

It was a couple minutes before Leroy was strong enough to return to Katie. She was sitting motionless in the same pose she had when he left the room. Her eyes were glassy as she gazed at the braided rug on the floor in front of her. When she heard her father return, she looked up. "It's okay, Daed. I'll be all right. Please don't worry."

"Oh, *liebschen*. Sweet Katie." He knelt beside her and placed his head in her lap and wept. Katie ran her fingers through his long hair as her tears dripped down, anointing him.

"I know God will make me better, Daed."

"Jah, oh, jah. We will pray every day—every hour for you to be healed, dochder. My little *wootzer.*" It had been years since he called her his little piggy. She had hated the name, but somehow it was reassuring to hear it today. She wanted to curl up into his lap and feel his protection overwhelm her, just as she had as a little girl. But now she found herself trying to comfort him. How strange, and yet she felt strength coming from somewhere. Somewhere above. She knew it was God. He was touching her, supporting her. Jah, she'd make it through this with His help and the love of her family. Oh, if only she had Josiah for support, but it wasn't to be. Nee, she'd get through it without him. God and God alone would be her resting place.

Holmes County, Ohio

Nellie watched her sister as she folded her dresses and placed them into the suitcase, so recently stored away. "I hope you don't have to stay too long."

"Jah, me, too. I think Mamm and Daed were getting over everything and I was beginning to feel really at home again."

101

"And Jeff's going to miss you," Nellie added, glancing over at her sister.

"So will Carrie."

"Jah, but Jeff even more."

"Don't go telling anyone about Jeff, Nellie. You promised."

"I'll be gut. Are you gonna go out with those kids when you have a chance? The ones who took drugs?"

"Of course not. I'm not there to socialize, Nell. I'm there to help."

"Jah, but you were there to help last time, too, but look what happened."

"It's totally different now. I've changed. I guess I've matured. Anyway, whatever I've done, I don't feel the need to party anymore."

"I bet it's because you love Jeff now, so other guys are boring."

"Maybe that's it. So, I think I have enough packed." She stood back and scanned the contents. "Maybe one more apron." She removed a black apron from a peg on the bedroom wall and laid it on the bed to pack.

"Do you have a picture of Jeff?"

"Actually, I do, but don't tell Mamm. She'd be mad."

"Are you taking it?"

"Of course! It was the first thing I packed. Oh, Nell, I'm gonna miss him so much."

"And me?"

Belinda sat on the bed next to her and put her arm around her. "Especially you."

"I'm sorry I was kinda mean when you first came home. You're not really a bad person. I was just mad because I thought you didn't care about being Amish anymore."

Belinda pulled back. No one knew her plans to become a Mennonite yet, not even Nellie. This was not the time to tell her.

"I'm sorry I disappointed you, Nell. And I shouldn't have sworn you to secrecy about my sneaking out at night. That wasn't fair. Forgiven?"

"Jah. Sisters forever, right?" She grinned at Belinda and they hugged each other.

"Will you write to me?" Belinda asked as she rose and snapped her suitcase shut before lowering it to the floor.

"You write first. Then I'll write back."

"Okay. I may be too busy in the beginning. I hope Wayne doesn't still like me."

"You didn't tell me about him. How do you know he liked you?"

"It was pretty obvious, but I didn't encourage him. Not once I knew Katie's best friend liked him. I didn't want to start trouble."

"I remember him. He was nice. Maybe I'll go out with him."

"You're only fifteen."

"So? He's not that much older. I think I'll go with you guys tomorrow so I can see him again."

"That's not going to happen."

"If I ask Mamm, she'll let me go."

"Nellie! Don't you dare!"

Nellie giggled and lay back on the bed. "I'm just teasing. I'm in love already, anyway."

Belinda grinned at her sister. "In love? My goodness. Who's the lucky guy?"

"Never mind. You don't even know him."

"Come on. You know about Jeff, so what's your boyfriend's name?"

"I guess I can tell you. Jonas Yoder."

"I know him. He's Lou Yoder's younger brother, right?"

"Jah. Of course, he doesn't know I like him. He barely talks to me, but I know I'll marry him someday."

"Goodness, you're pretty sure of yourself."

"Well, I'm pretty and smart and guys look at me a lot."

"You, my dear, are proud! Very, very proud and that is a no-no for a gut Amish girl."

"Maybe so, but you'll see. He's gonna notice me next year when I turn sixteen and go to the Sings."

"Don't rush it, Nellie. Men can be annoying."

"Is Jeff?"

"Nee. Not him. He's perfect."

"Oh, brother. Listen to you."

"Girls, food's on the table," Grace called up the stairs.

They walked arm and arm down the hallway toward the stairs. "I hope we'll be neighbors someday," Belinda said to her sister. "And we'll raise our families together."

"Jah, that would be ever so gut."

Belinda smiled as her family gathered for their meal. She was grateful God placed her in this loving Amish family. *Got is gut.*

Chapter Fifteen
Lancaster County, Pennsylvania

Leroy made his way slowly up the stairs to Mary and their bedroom. His wife was crocheting potholders for Christmas with three pillows shoved behind her back to raise her to a sitting position. She looked up as he entered.

"Leroy, you look like you've seen a ghost. What is it?"

He sat on the bed beside her and took her hand. She laid the potholder aside, feeling a sense of panic rise in her body. What could be so serious?

"Honey, the doctor stopped by a couple minutes ago to talk to us."

"Mercy, did they discover I have tuberculosis or something?" She lifted herself off the pillows and moved her legs to sit upright.

"Nee. It was about our Katie."

"What about her?"

"Mary, he said she's real sick. She has leukemia."

Mary pulled in a gasp of air. "Oh, dear God! Nee. It can't be. She's not that sick. Look at all the work she does, surely—"

"Honey, listen to me. The blood tests came back and they show she has it. They're going to do further testing Monday. He said they can probably stop it from getting worse. At least I think that's what he said."

"Why didn't you call me down? I should have been there. Sometimes you get things confused."

"I'm not confused, Mary. I know what he said and it ain't gut. We have to think positive though. They have drugs now that really help. He said they even have medicine you can take with water."

"Oh, Leroy. Tell me the truth. What are…?"

"Her chances? Honey, I don't know. It sounded like she could get through this and live okay, but right now she has to take it easy. He said the disease is draining her body."

"Poor, poor Katie. My darling boppli. How can this be? She seemed fine, just a little bit tired, is all. Please send her up. I need to hold my Katie." Mary burst into tears and Leroy surrounded her with his gentle arms and held her closely, his own tears blending with hers.

"We have to be strong, Mary. We have to help our dochder get through this. It's not going to be easy."

"What about Mamm? Can Belinda handle her by herself? We'll have to get Ruthie and Emma to come and help. Maybe Hannah and Fannie can give us a hand sometimes, too, even though they have their boppli to care for."

"Jah, they'll help I'm sure. They're gut daughters-in-law. It will take somebody to organize it, I'm thinking."

"What are they going to do Monday again?"

"Something about a bone marrow test. I don't know what it means, but it don't sound too gut."

"Oh, Leroy, Leroy, how can we manage everything that's happening to us? Why is everything so bad all of a sudden?"

"Honey, don't. We'll get through all this. Don't you worry. Remember we have God in our lives. He's always with us, gut days and bad."

"Jah. You're right. You're always right. What would I do without you?"

She leaned against his chest and closed her sore eyes. "I have to get better quick. Katie needs her mamm, and Oma needs her dochder. I really don't want her to go into a nursing home."

"Nee, we'll manage. Wayne can handle the farming once we finish the harvesting. Then I can help you out more here."

She moved away slightly and looked up at him. "Mamm is too modest to let a man help with some things."

"The personal stuff you girls can do, but we can help lift her and walk with her—things like that. Wayne can learn to hang clothes out, if he's needed."

"Mercy, he'd rather spend time in jail than do the wash."

"Let me go see if Katie's up to coming up here. She was just sitting quiet-like and praying when I left her."

"My poor dear Katie. My heart breaks for her. Jah, send her up."

Leroy told Katie her mother wanted to speak with her and she made her way slowly upstairs, supporting herself with the railing. She was so weak—even more so after hearing the doctor's report. When she came in the room, her mother stretched her arms out for her and Katie welcomed the embrace. Her love for her mother nearly overwhelmed her and she felt more sorrow for her mother than for herself. If she didn't conquer this illness, she'd be in Heaven with her Lord, but her mother would have the grief—the terrible heartache of losing her youngest daughter. *Lord, if for no other reason, please cure me for the sake of my parents.*

Holmes County, Ohio

"Daed spoke with the Bishop and he's relaxing his rules about the cell phone use. Because you're going to be so far, we can call you and receive calls from you." Grace pulled her shawl closer to her body as she watched Jeff place the suitcase and a tin with brownies into the trunk. It was getting cooler out and this morning was perfect weather for their trip to Pennsylvania. Clear skies and the promise of pleasant temperatures. She had discussed using a regular driver with Jed, but he seemed determined to stick with his plan to have Jeff drive their daughter. Encouraging the boy too much, she thought, but she accepted his choice—as she accepted most of his decisions. At least he seemed to have good character, for an Englisher.

"Then I'll call you tonight to let you know everything's all right." The family had all gathered to say good-bye, yet again. This time it was voluntary for Belinda, which made it an easier departure, and Grace hoped it wouldn't be as long this time. Her brother Gabe would be surprised to see Belinda back. He had a phone now, so she could call him to tell him, but perhaps his wife, Emma, already knew. News like this travels quickly in the Amish community. Emma was busy now with the twins, as well as Gabe's older two. Nice girl. Gabe was fortunate to find a woman like her after losing his first wife.

Jed hugged his daughter. "Don't work too hard. We'll need you back here." He gave her a forced grin.

"I'll miss you, Daed. You can write, you know."

"I'll leave that up to Nellie. She's the writer in the family."

Nellie nodded. "I'm gonna write a book someday."

"Well start with a letter," Grace said. "You write better than I do. Your printing is real nice."

"I can't write at all," Gideon added. "My teacher used to yell at me all the time."

"She didn't yell," Belinda said. "You always make stuff up about her. Take care, Gideon. Don't let the girls catch you."

"Ha. Ha. Yah, you too. Don't get drunk."

"Mercy, what a thing to say!" Grace scowled over at him.

Belinda gave everyone a hug and then climbed in the front seat and waited while Jeff shook hands with everyone. Then he got in and started the engine. He drove slowly down the drive as she hung her head out the window to wave.

Grace stood watching even as the others went back to the house. Since there was no service this Sunday, they planned to visit friends. She was glad she'd be busy. It would give her less time to ponder her daughter's future. It was obvious now that Belinda had strong feelings for Jeff and he, for her. As much as they attempted to appear as just friends, she caught their occasional exchange of words, which hinted at a deeper emotion than friendship. She would ask Jed to discuss it with the bishop before it went too far. Maybe their bishop could talk some sense into Belinda before things became serious.

Well, she was not going to worry anymore. There was no sense to it. She'd continue to pray about it and if it was the Lord's will for her daughter to marry outside the Amish, she'd have to accept it, but she could never shun her own child. Never in a million years. Thank goodness Belinda hadn't taken her vows yet.

When Grace walked into the kitchen, she found Jed and Gideon devouring the freshly baked sticky buns. She smiled over at her men. "Gut?"

"You make the best, Mamm," Gideon mumbled as he chewed a large hunk.

"Jah, she does," Jed agreed.

Nellie came in from the yard. "Hey, save some for me," she called out. "I get Belinda's piece, too."

"Oh, my, this family has a sweet tooth, that's for sure and for certain." Grace smiled as she reached for the coffee pot and sat down for her own goody. She checked her watch. It would be hours before they'd get a call from Belinda. In the meantime, she'd pray for her daughter's safety.

Chapter Sixteen
Between Counties

"You're awfully quiet," Jeff said as he drove onto the highway and set his car on cruise control. "You haven't said more than three words. Are you upset about leaving?"

"Well, jah. More upset than you are, I can see."

"Belinda, how can you say that? I'm just trying to deal with my feelings. It wouldn't help to act miserable."

A puff of air escaped her lips. "It might help me if I thought you were going to miss me."

He reached for her hand. "I dread being apart from you. You can't imagine how much I'll miss you, but I know you really didn't have a choice."

"Nee, I didn't. I'd feel guilty if I didn't go when they needed me like this. I wish they didn't have so many new boppli in the family. Then maybe they'd be able to pitch in and I wouldn't have to be there to help. Oh, well, it's only for a couple weeks until Katie's mamm is well enough to step in again. I'm sure Katie's tired, but she's young and all. If I give her a couple days of help, she'll probably snap right back. If things improve enough, would you be able to pick me up in two weeks?"

"Anytime. Tomorrow, if you can come home."

Belinda laughed. "I don't think that will happen, but if I know you're able to get me whenever I'm ready to return, that would help."

"I talked to my boss yesterday, just to tell him I might be a little late Monday morning. Depends on what time I get back tonight, and he said not to worry. Monday was going to be slow. Mainly inventory check and paper work."

"Maybe you can leave tomorrow morning then. You could get up early, but that way it wouldn't be so much driving in one day."

"That might work. Do you think they'd mind? I could sleep in the barn."

"I'm sure they wouldn't mind, and Wayne has room for you. That way we can spend more time together. Oh, Jeff, I'm gonna miss you so much." She lifted his hand and held it against her cheek.

"You're adorable. I love you so much," he said, smiling over.

"Me, too. Watch the road," she cautioned.

He continued to hold her hand until they came to an exit where they stopped long enough to use the facilities and fill the tank.

Normally, she and Jeff talked continuously, but today, they found it difficult to say much and instead drank in the beauty of the landscape and the comfortable relationship they had with each other. It wasn't necessary to fill the air with words. Unspoken messages came through as they touched briefly or exchanged smiles. Belinda knew she had found the love of her life.

Lancaster County, Pennsylvania

Katie sat sipping tea with her father while Oma napped. Mary was resting upstairs when Wayne appeared at the backdoor to announce the arrival of Belinda and Jeff. Normally cheerful, his eyes now held a note of sadness whenever he looked at Katie.

Dear Wayne. A man of few words—with her anyway, but his expression told it all. He was hurting, too. As small children, she and Wayne had played constantly together. He had taught her how to bait a hook, find the best hiding

112

places in the barn, even how to pitch a ball. He'd been her companion and their love for each other was strong. Jah, he was upset at the news, but when she told him, he had merely touched her cheek with his hand and shaken his head. "I'm sorry, Katie-girl." It was enough. It said it all. He loved her and it pained him to know she was so sick.

"You stay here, Katie," Leroy said as he arose from the table. "We'll greet them. Is she taking the dawdi haus again?"

"Jah, she may as well. She'll have her own bathroom and all. The bed's been made up. Daed?"

"Jah?"

"Let me tell Belinda—and the rest of the family, okay?"

"Sure, honey. If that's the way you want it."

"And I don't want everyone to know yet. Please don't tell other people."

"I won't. It will be up to you, Katie, but it's nothing to be ashamed about. You know that."

"It's not shame. I just don't want Josiah to find out."

He looked puzzled, but nodded in agreement as he made his way out the door.

Belinda came in to the kitchen a few minutes later, carrying a tin. "Hi, Katie. Mamm made brownies for you and all."

Katie smiled, gave her a hug, and took the tin from her hands. "Oh, I love brownies. Danki."

"You're real pale, Katie. I'm sorry you're not feeling so gut."

"Well, now that you're here, I can rest a bit. We really appreciate you coming out to help. My schwesters will help out, too, whenever they can."

"I know they will. How are Aenti Emma's twins?"

"Gut. Adorable, but they still get her up every couple hours at night. Poor Emma looks awful tired."

"I'm sure she is. Where should I sleep?"

"You can have the dawdi haus. It's all redded up for you."

"Danki."

Jeff appeared with the suitcase and was directed to Belinda's quarters after greeting Katie.

"If Jeff stays the night, can he sleep with Wayne?" Belinda asked as he disappeared into the other section of the house.

"Sure. Wayne won't mind. He likes Jeff."

"It's a long drive and he can leave early tomorrow and still get to work."

"He's a nice friend. You're lucky to have him."

Belinda grinned. "Jah. Very nice."

Oma called out from her bedroom and Katie and Belinda went in to see her and take care of her needs.

"Well, here's my little nurse back to help. What a nice sight. Come give me a kiss." Oma stretched out her arms.

Belinda bent over and kissed the elderly woman's cheek. The familiar scent of lavender filled her nostrils and she smiled at the sweet lady. "You look gut, Oma. Are you getting stronger?"

"Umm. I don't know. Am I, Katie?"

"Slowly, Oma. It takes time. We need to get you up more often though. That's the only way you'll get your strength back."

"Oh, jah, but it hurts sometimes. We'll see. I'm trying. So how are things in Ohio, Belinda?"

"Same as always. Busy. The crops were great this year. Just the right amount of rain and sun."

"Jah, I hear it was the same here. Lots of happy farmers."

After helping Oma to the bathroom, they led her into the living room where she sat to enjoy the family. After an hour passed, Ruth and Jeremiah showed up with baby Nathanael. Ruth's pregnancy was advancing into the last trimester and she grimaced as she leaned over to lift the baby from his car seat. "Just my back again," she explained when she saw Katie's expression.

A few minutes later, Emma and Gabe arrived with their four children and everyone greeted each other with hugs and smiles. It helped Belinda to feel the warmth of her extended family. Though she had not anticipated returning so quickly, she felt more content with her decision as she sensed their love for her as well as their appreciation.

Jeff seemed to fit right in and he and the men stood out on the porch to discuss the crops, the local news, and the price of goods. Belinda looked out and pretended they were already married. She visualized herself with a baby bump and a thrill went through her. She couldn't wait to have Jeff as her husband and have her own home and boppli someday.

Mary called down the stairs anxious to join her family. Leroy asked the girls to set up one of the upholstered chairs in the living room with extra pillows before helping her down to join the family. Ruth and Emma exchanged glances when they saw their mother, so frail, being led to her chair. Unbeknownst to the girls, not only her illness, but the strain of Katie's diagnosis, had taken its toll on their mother.

"Are our brothers coming by today?" asked Ruthie as she tucked a quilt around her mother's small frame.

"Nee, they're all off visiting Hannah's family. It's her mudder's birthday today."

"I haven't seen them in several weeks. I heard Hannah's expecting again," Ruthie said.

"Jah, Joseph's almost two. It was time, I guess," Mary said.

Belinda sat on the sofa next to Katie. She looked over at her. "You must be busy, planning your wedding. Have you set the date yet?"

Katie blanched. Her eyes were about to give her away, but she held back her tears and shrugged. "Not yet. I think we'll hold off till next year, with Oma and all."

Oma looked up, her mouth dropping open. "Katie, you were gonna live in the dawdi haus. You shouldn't delay your wedding on account of me."

"There are other things, too. I know what we said, but we should wait until we can move into our own place. Besides..."

"Jah, what?" Emma asked her sister.

"I ain't feeling all that gut, and a bride should be in gut shape."

Mary put her head down and dabbed her eyes with her apron.

Ruth looked at her mother and then turned to Katie. "Why is everyone upset? What's going on here?"

Katie put her head in her hands and then, taking a deep breath, sat back and spoke in quiet tones. "I'm real sick. I have leukemia."

"Oh, my God," Ruthie said, staring in disbelief.

Emma, who was nursing one of her twins, lifted her baby away from her breast and held her on her shoulder. "Katie, nee! It can't be. You're so young."

Mary allowed the tears to flow. "Your schwester is very brave. She's handling this better than Daed and me. The doctor wants to do more testing and then they'll figure out what kind of treatment she'll need."

Belinda sat silent, the impact of this news hitting her by degrees. Poor Katie. And her wedding was postponed.

Why would Josiah not insist on going through with the marriage as planned so he could be there to support her through this terrible time?

"Oh, Katie, I'm so sorry," Emma said as tears flowed down her cheeks. "We'll pray for you. God will cure you. I know it."

"Whatever is His will, Emma. I have to accept it."

Emma nodded, as she lowered her eyes.

Ruthie wiped her tears with a tissue and patted her growing abdomen as if to be reassured that part of her life was still all right. "What can we do to help you, Katie?"

"Just your prayers at this point. Maybe you can help Belinda. It's a lot for one person."

Oma blew her nose and looked over at Ruthie. "I don't need a bath every day and I'll do my therapy two times every day to get stronger faster. I hate being a burden. Maybe I should go to a nursing home. They can't be that bad and I have some money."

Mary looked over and shook her head. "Nee, Mamm. We will take care of you. Between all of us, you'll be fine. You're not a burden."

Belinda spoke up. "I like taking care of you. You're real easy and it's not too much work. I can do it by myself if no one else is here."

"You're a sweet angel of a girl," Oma said, smiling. "If the gut Lord takes me today, I would be just fine with it, so don't fret if my time comes soon."

Mary looked over and burst into fresh tears. "Oh my, Katie and Mamm, and me feeling so miserable." She began to cough and covered her mouth to avoid spreading the germs.

Jeff walked in at that moment and looked around at all the tears and broken hearts.

"I guess...I think...I'll come back later." He turned and headed out the door.

Belinda stood up. "I'd better go explain, if that's okay," she asked Mary.

"Of course. I thought Leroy was gonna tell the menfolk. You can suggest he do that, Belinda. Wayne's going to ride over to his bruders' homes tonight to tell them."

Katie spoke up. "I have one request of everyone. Please don't let this get out of the family right now. There are some people I don't want to know."

"Whatever you want, Katie," Ruthie said as the others nodded in agreement.

Belinda touched Katie on the shoulder as she passed by her chair on the way out. Then she stood on the back porch and motioned over to Jeff. He left the group of men and went to her. "What's wrong, Belinda. Is it your Aunt Mary?"

"Nee. It's Katie. She's real sick. I can't believe it—she has leukemia."

"Leukemia? Whoa. That's bad. No wonder they need your help."

"They just found out. She has to have more tests before they decide how to treat it. She's postponed her marriage, too. I guess it's too much to handle all at once."

"Josiah must be devastated."

"He doesn't know yet."

"Poor guy. I can't imagine..."

"I know. I feel so bad for everyone. And with her mudder so sick and Oma? It's an awful lot to bear."

"They'll have to lean on God to get them through all this. Thank goodness they're strong believers."

Belinda nodded. "Katie is amazing. She's the strongest of all. I have a lot of respect for her, Jeff. I didn't give her credit for being such a gut person."

"She'll need to rest when she gets treated. Her body is probably weakened from the disease. It's going to be a lot for you, Belinda. Think you can handle it by yourself?"

"I don't have much choice, though everyone's going to try to pitch in."

"Maybe I can come up some week-end and bring Carrie or Nellie to help."

"Carrie's just started college. Maybe Nellie, though. I'll probably be here longer than I'd hoped, Jeff. I hope you understand."

"Honey, of course I do. Would it be too much on everyone if I do come sometimes?"

"I'm sure they'd be fine with it. You can help the guys with the farming."

"I'd like that, and of course, I'd see you. Maybe we can talk by phone at night when we're apart."

"I don't have my own phone."

"I'll buy you one and bring it next time."

"Oh, Jeff, that's sweet of you, but I don't think I can afford to service one."

"I'll put you on our family plan and pay for it myself. I have to be able to talk to you, Belinda. It's gonna be hard enough not seeing you. At least this way we can keep in touch."

"If it's not too expensive, I guess it will be okay. After all, this is kind of an emergency situation. I don't think the bishop would object."

"Honey, soon it won't matter what the bishop thinks. You'll be free to do as you please, remember?"

She shook her head. "It's hard for me to think of being anything besides Amish. My heart—"

"I know, you're Amish through and through," he said with a grin. "But your values and beliefs won't change.

You'll just put on a different cap and maybe different clothes and be cool in the summer."

She smiled and reached for his hand. "You make it sound easy."

"It will be when you're Mrs. Jeffrey Richardson."

"Sounds so gut. Oh, Jeff. It seems like a long way away."

"Maybe only a year. Let's see how it goes. I need to be able to provide for my wife."

"I don't need much to be happy."

"No, but it helps to have a roof over your head."

"Jah, and maybe some food in my tummy."

He smiled and leaned over to kiss her on her nose. "I can't wait."

They began to walk toward the barn. Belinda noticed the men had circled together—arms around each other's shoulders, obviously in prayer. "Wait, Jeff. I think Leroy has told the others about Katie. Let's give them privacy."

He nodded and they walked quietly out of sight of the house and the men. When they reached the horse corral, they stopped and rested against the fence. "I know they've come a long way in treating leukemia, Belinda. If they caught it early enough, she probably stands a good chance of beating it. I guess you're never actually cured, but if it's dormant you can live a normal life. My mother had a friend whose son had leukemia."

"There are different kinds, aren't there?"

"Yeah. That's what I've heard. You'll learn more once she's tested further, I'm sure."

"Would you marry me if I had something like that?"

He put his arms around her. "I'd marry you no matter what happened to you. What difference would it make if you got sick?"

"What if I couldn't have children?"

"Honey," he moved back and lifted her chin. "Nothing would keep me from wanting you as my wife. Nothing." Then he leaned over and kissed her gently on her lips. When he moved back, she smiled at him.

"I can't believe I'm engaged to such a wonderful-gut person. God is smiling upon me."

"Upon us."

They patted a horse's head after he sidled up to the fence. "Did you have a chance to ask about my staying tonight? Maybe with everything that's going on, I should head back to Ohio today."

"Nee. I have it all taken care of. You'll sleep with Wayne. He has the extra bed."

"Wayne's a good guy. We get along pretty well. I wonder how he's handling Katie's illness. Apparently they're close."

"He probably keeps his feelings hidden, but I'm sure it's tough on him, too."

"Think we should go back in?" Jeff asked.

"Probably, but I think I need one more kiss. A week's a long time."

He immediately surrounded her with his arms and after a passionate kiss, she moved back and let out a low whistle. "My goodness, you take my breath away."

He grinned, took her hand, and they returned to the farmhouse.

In spite of the dark cloud over this family, Belinda saw their amazing support for each other as well as their resilience. God was working.

Chapter Seventeen
Lancaster County, Pennsylvania

Katie sat with her father in the waiting room. Mary had stayed home to rest. Though she was feeling somewhat better now that the antibiotics were beginning to work, she was still extremely weak. Leroy was adamant about following the doctor's orders regarding her bed rest.

Dr. Humphrey's nurse led them into an examination room where they waited an additional ten minutes before a middle-aged, sandy-haired man came through the door wearing a white lab coat. He extended his hand and introduced himself as the oncologist. Taking a seat behind his desk, he opened her chart. After a few moments he spoke. "Your doctor has told you the diagnosis?" He looked directly at Katie.

"Jah. I mean, yes."

"Did he explain we need to take some bone marrow to learn more about your condition?"

Katie nodded. She felt perspiration forming under her arms as she shuffled her feet.

"I'm sorry you have to go through this, Kate, but it's necessary so we can determine the extent of the disease and plan for your recovery."

"I understand."

Leroy ran his hands through his hair. "Will it hurt my daughter a lot?"

"No, we'll just aspirate a section of bone to obtain the marrow. It's a quick procedure. There are several types of leukemia, so first we must determine what type we're dealing with. This is one of our tools. Well, young lady, I'll have the nurse help you change and I'll be right back. I can answer your questions after I have answers."

Leroy went back to the waiting room and tried to read a magazine. The words danced before his eyes without his comprehension. He laid it back down and began pacing. The receptionist smiled at him. It was difficult to return her smile, though he made a weak effort. An elderly man was stretched out on one of the leather seats, eyes closed, and unmoving—probably asleep.

His little girl, his Katie, was struggling for her life. Oh, how he wished he could take it from her—even if it meant taking on the disease himself. She was so special to him, not that the others weren't loved equally, but she was the happy child. The one always with a smile for her daed—following him around as he milked the cows or fed the goats. She used to sing. Sweet happy sounds. Her Jesus songs, as she called them. He pictured her the day she learned to skip. She finally caught on as she tried to mimic her older sisters, Ruth and Emma. It was a struggle, but then she mastered it. She skipped for two days straight—everywhere she went. And always a grin. *Dear God in heaven. Please spare my little girl's life. Don't let her suffer, God. Please.*

It seemed to take forever, but only an hour had passed. Then the nurse came out to get him and he followed her back to the same room where Katie sat, fully dressed, waiting for instructions. The nurse wrote something on her chart and then told them to make an appointment for the following Friday. "We should have the results by then. At the next visit, the doctor will discuss the therapy appropriate for your type of leukemia."

Katie bit her lip and then spoke softly. "Do you think I'm going to die soon?"

"Oh, Kate, we can't make that determination," the nurse started saying. Then she stopped and laid a hand on Katie's arm. "Dear, we help many patients here with all types and stages of cancer. I'm sure we can help you. Our goal is to get you into remission. We may not be able to cure you, but you can live a good life with proper treatment. The doctor will be able to give you a full report when he sees you next time. Right now you need to get rest and eat properly. Try to get some exercise also, but not to the point of exhaustion. Your body will be working with us to get you through this, so we need to treat it with respect. Okay?"

Katie nodded. "I'll try to do whatever I can. Thank you."

On the way home in the buggy, Katie attempted to have a light conversation. She talked about the falling leaves and how she'd loved jumping in them when she was little. "My students loved this time of year."

"Do you miss teaching, Katie?" Leroy asked.

"A little. I thought I'd be getting married after I quit, but I realize it would have been way too much for Mamm to take care of Oma by herself."

"You can still get married, honey." He looked over at Katie to watch her reaction.

She put her head down. "I'm not engaged anymore, Daed."

"What? You broke off with Josiah?" His mouth dropped open as he waited for her answer.

"I broke off with him a few days ago. I don't want to see him again—ever."

"Katie, you seemed so happy together. What happened to change all that?"

"I can't tell you everything, Daed. Sometimes I'm not even sure myself what happened, but I can tell you this. The way I feel, I'll never go back to him."

"Well, I'm sorry to hear that, Katie. Real sorry. I thought he was a pretty nice Amish man. He sure seemed to care for you."

"Don't Daed. I don't want to talk about it anymore. I have enough on my mind."

"Jah, you do, honey. Too much, if you ask me."

"Daed, I don't want anyone to tell my friends about this leukemia. Especially Josiah. He might feel bad and want to come back to me, but it would be out of pity and if there's anything I don't want, it's that."

Leroy nodded. He slackened the reins and allowed the horse to lead the way at his own pace. "What if it wasn't pity, Katie? What if it was out of love?"

"Nee. Please. I can't deal with this. I have too many maybes in my life right now. I'm so tired. I just want to go home and lie down."

"Jah, I don't blame you. We'll be home shortly." He lifted the reins and clucked to encourage his faithful horse to return home a wee bit faster. A nap would feel mighty gut about now for him, too.

Josiah laid his paintbrush out on the porch after rinsing it out. The incentive to work on the house was gone, but at least he'd finish painting the guest room. The rest could wait. A long time. There was absolutely no hurry for anything anymore. Not without Katie.

Whatever happened to make her so angry? Jah, Priscilla was a factor. It probably looked like a lot more was going on than it was. Sure, she's pretty and likes to flirt, but he would never leave his Katie for her or any other woman. Why would she think that?

If only he had spent more evenings with Katie, even if she was pre-occupied with her grandmother's care. Eventually, she would have found more time for him. It was immature of him to expect her full attention when she had the responsibility for her grossmammi. It should have been enough for him to just see her and talk to her. But nee, he had to have her all to himself. Guilt rose in him. It was not a Godly way to behave. If only he could do it over.

Tonight, he'd go over and try to get her to listen. He'd explain again that Priscilla was merely a friend. They only played board games a couple times, and only at her insistence. It's not like he initiated anything, because he didn't. He might have been attracted a year ago, but not since falling in love with Katie. She was the only girl for him and even if she refused to get together again with him, she would still be the one for him. He'd wait. He'd wait as long as it took. He had to convince her of his love—that was for sure. So tonight, after a hot shower and a light meal, he'd head over and clear things up. Once and for all. Tonight, they'd set a date for their wedding and nothing— and no one—would stand in their way!

Chapter Eighteen
Holmes County, Ohio

"I can't believe it," Carrie said as she pulled the lettuce apart for salad. "Poor girl. Leukemia. Belinda's going to be exhausted with all that sickness going on there. Maybe next week-end I can go with you, Jeff, and help out."

"I was surprised to see you come home from college this week-end. Bored already?"

"No, just homesick. It's good to get away from the crowds, too. In fact, I'm going to come home most week-ends."

"Unless you find a new guy to pursue?" Jeff placed a handful of silverware on the patio table and went over to the grill to check the burgers. "I meant to ask you about Dan. Still seeing him?"

"Not for a while. He comes on pretty strong."

"I warned you."

"I still kind of like him, but I'm uneasy around him. Look, I'm serious about next weekend. Do you think they'd mind if I tagged along? I could be a real help, you know."

"I think Belinda would be pleased to have the extra hands and I can always hang out with Wayne or her father when she's too busy to see me."

"It's gotta be hard on you, too, bro." Carrie slid the cut up tomatoes and onions into the salad bowl. "How are the burgers?"

"Nearly done. I'll talk to Belinda and ask if it would be okay for both of us to come out there. It's a long drive."

"I don't care. I'd love to see her as well. We got pretty close you know."

"Yeah, I know."

"When is she going to tell her parents about you two?"

"It can wait awhile. I think her dad will be okay, but her mother resents me sometimes, even though it's not like she'll lose her daughter when we get married."

"She might. They could ban Belinda. Even if they don't go that far, her mother may be fearful that the community won't mean as much to Belinda if she starts going to the Mennonite services and all. I can see where it might bother her."

"Mmm. I guess. So you can call the folks. Burgers are just about ready."

Carrie went inside to get her parents. Jeff looked at his watch. Good, it was almost time to call Belinda—the highlight of his day. He was glad he had sent her new phone overnight express. It was worth the money to be able to speak to her every night. Sometimes the poor girl was so tired, she'd fall asleep while they were talking. By the time she was done with all her chores, it was usually nine o'clock in the evening and rising before six made for a short night.

Belinda was delighted to know Carrie would be willing to help. After getting the okay from the family, she called back and they made their arrangements for the weekend. When they said good night, it was nearly ten o'clock. Jeff could hear her yawning in the phone. "Good night, sleepyhead," he said. Then he went up to his room and started his homework. It would be a busy week, but studying helped pass the time.

Lancaster County, Pennsylvania

Katie went to bed right after she ate her supper. She was totally exhausted. The night sweats had increased and her sleep pattern was irregular, causing her eyes to look dull above the purple circles underlying them.

Shortly after she went upstairs, there was a knock on the front door. Leroy went to answer it. Josiah stood, hat in hand, waiting to be asked in. Leroy hesitated and then told him Katie was in bed.

"Already? It's only half past six. Is she just napping? I can wait for her to wake up."

"I don't think that's a gut idea, sohn. She's down for the night."

"Oh. Is she okay?"

"She's asleep."

"Jah, I figured. Well, will you tell her I came by? I need to talk to her. It's real important."

"I'll tell her."

He stood a moment longer. "Well, I guess I'll head home."

"That's a gut idea."

Josiah stood and turned his straw hat in his hand, not budging.

"So, I'm gonna close the door now," Leroy said, lowering his eyes.

"Oh. Jah. Have a nice night."

"Same to you, Josiah." Leroy slowly closed the door, while the young man remained in place. It certainly was an awkward moment, but Katie had sworn him to secrecy. She had enough stress without adding more right now. If the two of them were to patch up, then it could wait a couple more weeks.

It was time to return to the oncologist. This time Mary insisted on going along. She wanted to hear for herself about Katie's condition. Leroy didn't object since the medicine Mary was taking had finally kicked in and her coughing had subsided substantially.

Katie looked out at the landscape as their horse trotted along the side of the road. Her parents sat in front and spoke of the colorful fall. She wondered how many autumns she had left. Nee, that was negative thinking. She'd know more after today. Maybe they had made a mistake in her diagnosis. She felt sick, but not like she had something horrible like leukemia, for heaven's sake.

"Here we are, Katie. I'll let you two out and then take the buggy into the back."

Katie and her mother walked into the waiting room and gave Katie's name to the receptionist.

"Take a seat and we'll call you shortly."

Leroy came in a couple minutes later and took a seat beside his wife. They sat silently waiting for the nurse to appear. At last she led them back to the same examination room they'd had before, and Leroy stood against the wall as the women took seats in front of the desk. Dr. Humphrey came in and sat down after being introduced to Mary.

"I have the results of the biopsy and I'm glad to say you're in the early stage of chronic myeloid leukemia."

"That's gut?" Leroy asked, pulling on his suspenders. "It don't sound so gut."

"Well, if you have to have leukemia, at least it's treatable at this early stage. We can put your daughter on oral medicine and see how that works before trying chemo or anything more drastic. We'll have to keep a close eye on her, but side effects have been minimal in most of my patients who take the drug."

"Do I have to take it everyday?" Katie asked.

"Yes. It's unusual for a girl your age to have this type of leukemia, though not unheard of. We found the presence of Philadelphia chromosomes, which is indicative of CML."

"Philadelphia?" Mary asked. "Funny name for something so bad."

The doctor smiled for the first time. "I'm not sure how the gene mutation got that name, but yes, it is a strange name. Now we'll have to monitor Kate's organs while she undergoes treatment."

"You mean it's only for a little while?"

"Actually, it's long term. We'll order a TKI drug—that stands for tyrosine kinase inhibitor, before you leave the office and you can start it tomorrow. It may cause some minor anxiety or nausea, but after awhile, your body will probably tolerate it better. Questions?"

Katie looked down at her apron and pleated it while she asked her question. "Will I be able to have bop..babies?"

"Some women have delivered babies, though sometimes we see cases of infertility. If you do get pregnant, we suggest stopping the treatment temporarily. You run the risk of relapse, however."

"I see." Katie kept her head down, but she wiped at her eyes and had no further questions.

"Set up an appointment with the receptionist. I'd like to see Kate every week at first and then you can come less frequently after we have her established on the treatment." He stood and Kate and her mother rose also. Leroy shook the doctor's hand and nodded.

After filling the prescription, they rode home in silence. Katie's head was throbbing, she felt nauseated and she hadn't even had a dose yet. What was ahead for her? Infertility? What good was an Amish woman who couldn't have boppli?

As Leroy helped her down from the carriage, he remembered Josiah's visit. Somehow it didn't seem like the right time to mention the young man's appearance. The information could wait. Right now his daughter needed peace and rest. He was determined to provide both.

Chapter Nineteen
Holmes County, Ohio

Jeff checked his watch several times, anxious to start his trip to Pennsylvania. His last job was exhausting. Planting two-dozen eight-foot arborvitae along a property line with only one other guy to help was no easy task. Relieved that he finished the job before quitting time, he pushed the wheelbarrow with supplies over to his truck, as his helper watered the newly planted trees. They had arrived at the site in separate vehicles. Jeff left first. He could wait until the next morning to make his way to Pennsylvania, or he could take a rest and leave this evening. He opted for his second choice and drove slightly over the speed limit to reach his employer's business, where he parked the truck and unloaded. He picked up his paycheck and headed home.

Carrie had just arrived from college and waved as he pulled up. She seemed excited to be going to Pennsylvania with him and grinned as her brother exited his car, covered in dirt—sweat on his brow.

"You look like a real farmer, Jeff."

"Don't even talk about it. I'm beat. I'm gonna need an hour's rest after I shower and eat something and then we can take off."

"I thought you said we'd leave tomorrow."

"I suppose we could wait, but I'd rather get started tonight."

"It's okay. I can pack in ten minutes. I can help you drive, bro. My day was a lot easier than yours."

"That wouldn't be hard."

After grabbing a shower, a nap, and a turkey sandwich, Jeff threw some items into a backpack and reached for his sister's carry-on suitcase. She followed him out to the car and suggested she drive the first hour or two. He didn't object and climbed into the passenger seat while she got into the driver's side and turned the key in the ignition.

They headed out the drive. It was still light out and Jeff was glad they'd have a couple hours of daylight for their drive.

After a few minutes Carrie broached the subject of her relationship with Dan. "He called me again. I think I'll go out with him, as long as it's in a public place."

"That probably won't stop him," Jeff said, scowling.

"Goodness, you really don't like him, do you?"

"I don't like the fact that he's going out with my sister."

"I can handle him."

"Right."

"Jeff, he's really not that bad. He seems more ... I don't know, maybe reticent lately. Maybe he's growing up."

"Yeah. I'll believe it when I see it."

"Well, I'm not going to marry the guy, but he's fun to be with. Good for a laugh."

"Belinda found out otherwise."

"Belinda didn't know how to handle him. After all, she's not used to forward men."

"I guess not. You do what you want, Carrie, just remember I warned you."

"Oh, brothers. They're so over-protective."

"I talked with Belinda last night. Katie had a bone test and now she's being treated with an oral drug. I guess it was a relief not to need chemo."

"I'd imagine so. So they think it's curable?"

"Treatable and controllable. I don't think it's actually curable."

"That's such a shame. How old did you say she was?"

"Eighteen."

"Oh, wow. That's awful. Does she still live at home?"

"Yes. She was engaged, but Belinda said that's off."

"Through her choice?"

"I don't really know. Anyway, it's not going to be a fun week-end I'm afraid."

"I'm not coming along to have 'fun.' I miss Belinda and I'd like to help out while I'm there."

"You know, it might involve diaper changing?"

"There's a baby there?"

"I mean for the elderly woman. She's incontinent."

"What a shame. I can handle it. Remember I helped at the nursing home one summer?"

"I'd forgotten. Yeah, you're good with old people."

"I'm thinking about going into nursing."

"Again? You used to talk about it all the time."

"I was too young to make a final decision when I talked about it before. Now, though, I've had time to think about it and I believe God is directing me."

"Go for it. You'd be good. Did you tell the folks?"

"No, I just decided this last week. My roomy is a nursing student and I've been going through her books and talking to her. I think I'd be happy as a nurse. I know Mom will be okay about it."

"Not Dad?"

"I don't know. Maybe. I'm not sure he thinks I'm smart enough."

Jeff looked over at her profile. Was she serious? "Why would you think that?"

"Just that I mentioned it once and he laughed and said it was hard work and I'd be better off teaching school."

"Like teaching isn't hard."

"Yeah, right? And Mom being a teacher once, she wasn't too happy with his remark."

"He probably didn't mean anything by it."

"Maybe not. I'm too sensitive sometimes. So, have you and Belinda set a date at least to get engaged?"

"I think we already are engaged. I asked her and she said yes."

"No ring?"

"The Amish—"

"Oh, I forgot. So you just kind of agree."

"Pretty much. I still can't believe she loves me enough to marry me."

"Jeff, you're a great guy. Any girl would be pleased to marry a man like you."

"Yeah? That's the nicest thing you've ever said to me. Can't believe it."

"Oh, shush. I'm gonna pull over at the next rest stop and hand the wheel over to you."

"That's fine."

It helped to have company on his trip and he and Carrie had always been close. He was pleased his sister and future wife were also good friends. Things were going well. He glanced over once and Carrie was dozing. He took this opportunity to pray and thank God for bringing Belinda into his life and all the many blessings he had. The sky was pitch black now, the moon in its crescent shape. He enjoyed listening to the music and knowing that he would soon be with Belinda. Some day, he'd be with her every single day.

He couldn't wait. Maybe they could wed the following spring. It was time to set a date.

Lancaster County, Pennsylvania

Belinda turned down the bedding for Oma while Mary helped her mother brush her teeth. Belinda checked her watch. Jeff and Carrie should arrive around ten. Only three more hours. Her excitement at seeing them increased as the time got closer.

Several minutes later, they had Oma tucked in for the night and Mary left to sit with Leroy on the porch.

Oma patted Belinda's hand. "That young Englishman has a fancy for you, I'm thinking. Be careful, honey. Don't let him turn your head."

"Mmm. He's a real nice man. In fact he's going to be a Mennonite."

"Jah? My, my. Maybe you can get him to be Amish instead. Ain't that far apart."

"We'll see. Now you have a gut night and don't let the bugs bite."

"Mercy me," she laughed. "Nee, no bugs for me. Danki, Belinda. You're a sweet girl."

Belinda leaned over and kissed the woman's cheek. "That's a nice thing to say. You're a very special lady, you know."

"I'm too tired out to argue." She grinned and closed her eyes. Belinda lowered the shade and headed toward the kitchen.

Katie was sitting alone with a pot of fresh brewed tea beside her when Wayne walked in and glanced over at his sister. "Made enough for me to have a cup?"

"Plenty. You, too, Belinda, if you want one," she added as Belinda joined them.

"I could use a pick-me-up. Jeff and Carrie won't get here for a few more hours."

Wayne reached for two mugs and handed one to Belinda, setting the other on the table. They sat down as Katie poured. No one spoke for a couple moments while the sugar was passed.

"Who's Carrie?" Wayne asked, turning his head toward Belinda.

"Jeff's sister. She's my age."

He took a sip of tea and then set it down. "Does she live at home?"

"Actually, she's in college this year, but yes, she still lives at home. We're real gut friends."

"Was she the one who helped you get in trouble?"

Belinda giggled. "I didn't need any help, I'm afraid. She was one of my friends though. She's really a nice person. I think you'll like her."

Katie smiled for the first time. "Find me a girl my brother wouldn't like."

"Oh, come on, Katie. I'm not that girl-crazy."

"Jah, you are. And the girls like you."

"Not all of them." He frowned and added another spoonful of sugar.

"I know one who does," Belinda said. "Becky."

"Oh, jah, everyone wants me to go with Beck. Maybe if I didn't get pushed so much, I *would* like her."

"She's pretty and smart and cooks real gut," Katie said. "You could do worse, I'd say."

"I heard Pris called off her engagement with John. Maybe I'll take her to a Sing."

Katie's eyes filled. "I think it's too late."

"What do you mean?" he asked, his brows rose.

"Just that. I think she likes someone else already."

"Who?"

Katie felt a tear escape and make its way down her cheek. "Who? Just Josiah, that's who."

Wayne's mouth dropped open. "What's going on? You're not serious."

"Oh, no? I've never been more serious in my life. Jah, Josiah and I broke up. Priscilla can have him, the unfaithful—man!" Now her tears were uncontrolled.

Belinda was as shocked as Wayne. "I can't believe you two have broken up. Was it because of your illness?"

"He doesn't even know. And I don't want him to find out. Not a word! I don't want a man's pity and that's the only reason he'd come back to me now. I went over to see him last week and Priscilla came in right while I was there and it wasn't the first time she was alone in *our house* with him! He admitted she comes by to see him. You know what kind of girl she is, Wayne. Why would you even consider seeing her? So you see, you're too late anyway. Josiah can have her!" Katie put her head down in her arms and lay over on the table, nearly spilling her tea.

Belinda shoved it aside and moved over to put her arms around her. "No one will tell him a thing. That's terrible. I can't believe it."

Wayne finally found his voice. "I *don't* believe it. I know how much he loves you, Katie-girl." He patted the top of her head.

"Don't say 'loves.' Loved maybe, but not now. He just didn't want to wait for me. I guess it was too much to expect him to hang around until things got better here. Now they'll never be better. Oh, God, help me. I may never have boppli. This leukemia is ruining my life." She continued to weep, nearly uncontrollably now. Mary and Leroy came in from the back porch, alarmed by the sound of sobs coming from their daughter, who had appeared so strong earlier.

They all grouped together, touching Katie. Leroy prayed a blessing over her and pled for his daughter's life. Wayne wiped his eyes with his sleeve while Mary allowed her tears to moisten her daughter's kapp. It would get better. It had to. What was God's will for this family? Their faith never wavered, but so many questions went unanswered. At least, for now.

Chapter Twenty
Lancaster County, Pennsylvania

"And this is Wayne, Katie's brother," Belinda said to Carrie.

Wayne stood awkwardly as he nodded at the attractive English blonde, who extended her hand. Blush went up his neck and he avoided her eyes as he shook her slender hand. "Nice to meet you."

"Yeah, me, too." Carrie gave him a huge smile, weakening his knees even further and raising the crimson color to his hairline. Goodness, he didn't remember ever being this infatuated so immediately in all his eighteen years. It was at moments like this that he wished he were English!

"I know it's late," Belinda said, "but are you guys hungry?"

"I could eat," Jeff said. "I don't know about Carrie."

"There's homemade bologna in the fridge," Wayne announced. "I can make you sandwiches if you want."

Carrie tilted her head. "Don't tell me you make your own bologna."

"I helped," he said proudly. "I could make it myself, but my daed likes to do it."

"I could go for a half sandwich," she said in reply.

Belinda looked over at Jeff. "Do you want her other half plus a full one?"

"Sounds good. Thanks. I'm sorry we got in late. Traffic was bad tonight."

Belinda smiled at her fiancé. "I'm relieved you made it. I'm glad you called though or I would have been worried."

"There are advantages to some of the new technology."

"I wish I had my own phone," Wayne said as he pulled the meat and a container with cheese from the refrigerator. Belinda was amused. She'd never seen him do anything besides eat in their kitchen. She was sure Carrie had something to do with his sudden interest in hospitality. Now that was one relationship, which couldn't hatch. Carrie was so education-minded and sophisticated. Poor Wayne. He'd better stick to an Amish girl. They were just as intelligent, but lacked the higher education. Belinda had never desired to go further in her schooling, but she knew several others who resented the fact they were not even allowed to take college courses.

The four of them sat at the table and chatted quietly. Carrie's tight blouse embarrassed Belinda. She knew it would be difficult for Wayne to dismiss it from his mind. He appeared to avert his eyes every time he addressed the lovely English girl, but his constant flush told her he was very aware of her clothing. Amish girls had the right idea. Belinda never had to worry about guys getting the wrong impression by the way she dressed. It was fun to be feminine and modest at the same time. Another reason to remain Amish. Just maybe she could convince Jeff to take the next step and give up his car—even if it meant no air conditioning. That way, she wouldn't have to upset her family and she could teach him the *Ordnung*—the book of rules for living. They weren't that difficult once they were explained—at least not for someone who only knew that way of life. Jah, it might be hard for Jeff to adhere to so many restrictions. Maybe the Mennonite route was the way to go. Oh, such problems.

There was no opportunity to be alone with Jeff. Probably just as well. He looked so wonderful to her. She just wanted to be held in his arms. Not appropriate. How on earth were they going to wait another year or two? Mercy, it would be difficult.

He was able to sneak a quick kiss as she passed him later on her way to the dawdi haus with Carrie. Seconds later, her uncle appeared out of nowhere to check on everyone. Very close call. If it got back to her parents they were caught kissing, she'd probably be on probation for the rest of her life!

Early the next morning, Belinda prepared a breakfast of scrapple and eggs with homemade muffins for the men of the house. After Leroy and Wayne left for the barn, she checked on Oma, and then finding her still asleep, she returned to the kitchen where Jeff was preparing to join the men.

He stopped first and took her hands. "I've missed you so much. What are our chances of having a few minutes together—alone?"

"Probably not great, but I have to be with you before you head back tomorrow. Maybe after lunch, Katie can just sit with Oma and read to her or something to give me a break."

"Carrie will be there to help, too. You know she worked with old people one summer and liked it."

"I know, she mentioned going into nursing last night. I think she'd be a great nurse. Yah, maybe once Oma gets to know her a little better, I can get extra time off while she's still here. I really, really appreciate you guys doing this. I know it's a long drive for only a couple days."

"Oh, Belinda, if it meant being together only a couple hours, it would still be worth it. I've missed you so much."

"At least we talk everyday. That helps."

"Let me hold you just for a moment and then I'll go out and help."

She put her arms around his waist and soaked up his masculine scent while closing her eyes. He touched the back of her kapped head and kissed the side of her cheek. Then his lips met hers and for a brief moment they were immersed in a perfect kiss—gentle and sweet. My, what a fortunate woman she was.

Footsteps sounded on the stairway. He moved away, gave her an intimate smile, and headed out the back door.

She blew a kiss as he closed the screen door behind him.

Katie came through the hallway and into the kitchen just in time to wave to him. Then she poured a glass of juice and sat at the table. "Is Oma awake yet?"

"Nee. Carrie's still asleep, too. I didn't want to wake her yet."

"Of course not. It was nice of her to come and help. I think Wayne's glad she came." Katie wasn't smiling.

"Oh, most guys tend to act a little funny around her. She is pretty."

"Jah, she is. I wish she'd wear looser clothing though. Wayne ain't used to girls all fancy."

"I'll mention it to her. She probably has a sweater she could put on."

"If not, I have an extra shawl."

Belinda reached for a piece of cooled-off toast and spread it with homemade grape jelly.

Katie poured herself a glass of orange juice and sat back in her chair.

Belinda set her toast aside. "How are you feeling, Katie?"

"Tired is all. My nights are awful. I can hardly sleep with all the hot sweats I get."

"Goodness, that would be annoying. When do you start your medicine?"

"I already did."

"Does it affect you?"

"Not too bad. Once in awhile I feel woozy, but they gave me medicine for that, too." Katie turned her glass around and around, staring at the deep orange liquid.

"When will you know you're better?" Belinda asked softly.

"I don't know. I go every week for a while. I guess the doctor will check my blood often enough to know when I don't have to worry anymore."

"Katie, I'm sorry it didn't work out with you and Josiah. If you ever want to talk about it, I'm here for you."

A smile tucked at Katie's mouth. "Danki. I appreciate it, but I'll be all right. I have too much to think about to worry about a guy right now."

Belinda nodded, as she proceeded to finish the toast. "I'd better go check Oma when I'm done here. Why don't you let Carrie and me handle everything today? Maybe you can get a rest."

"Sometimes I think it's better to stay busy, though it's harder all the time to make those steps down to the basement."

"Then you can stay on this floor and read to Oma or help her with her quilting and Carrie and I will do the wash. Is there any laundry down there, which we should take care of?"

"Jah, Oma went through two sets of sheets yesterday. I have them soaking. Even with adult diapers…"

Mary came down the stairs just as Carrie entered the room in her short terry bathrobe. Mary let out a short gasp, but nodded a greeting to the girls. Carrie pulled her robe closer around her body and tightened the belt.

"Any men around?" Carrie asked the women.

"Not at the moment, but one could appear at any moment," Katie said, a scowl settling across her mouth.

Carrie looked over at her and shrugged. "I'll just grab a cup of java and go get dressed. Sorry I shook everyone up. I really didn't mean to. At home…"

"It's okay," Mary said, trying to smile. "It's just not the Amish way, is all, at least in our home. Little kinner sometimes run around in their jammies, but once a girl becomes…"

"Gotcha. I'll be right back." Carrie slipped back through the door to the dawdi-haus and came out a few minutes later in her jeans and a floppy sweatshirt. Not very feminine, but a better choice than the outfit she arrived in.

The day went swiftly. Katie and her mother sat with Oma and they sang together as they worked on the quilt. While they took care of Oma's needs, Carrie and Belinda did three loads of wash and hung them out to dry. Then they cleaned the first floor thoroughly with wet mops and a carpet sweeper. Dusting took longer, but when they were finished, the tables sparkled with a coating of fresh bees wax.

Late afternoon Mary felt well enough to start supper. Carrie took a few minutes to go over some homework while Belinda sat on the porch, folding towels and underwear.

Leroy, Wayne, and Jeff were in and out a few times, but finally Jeff and Belinda found themselves alone. Jeff sat on the porch step and leaned his head back. "Wow! I'm beat. These guys sure know how to work."

Belinda giggled. "Jah, Amish men ain't lazy, that's for sure."

"Aren't lazy."

"That's what I said. Oh, you don't like 'ain't?'"

"Well, it sounds cute coming from you, but it's poor grammar, you know."

"Sorry." Belinda looked down at the bath towel she was folding and smoothed it out on her lap, keeping her head lowered. His words had cut her. Apparently her speech embarrassed him.

"Honey, I'm sorry if I hurt you. I didn't mean to." He reached over with his hand and held it open for hers. Haltingly, she accepted his gesture and slipped her hand into his. He squeezed it. "Wanna go for a walk?"

"I'm too tired. Carrie just went in to study for a while. She's not used to working this hard either."

"When we're married, you can use a real vacuum and an automatic washer and dryer."

"Not the dryer. No way. I like my clothes to be air-dried. Ever so much nicer when they're dried by a fresh breeze."

"Maybe, but I can't imagine washing cloth diapers in those antique washers I've seen. Maybe we'll use disposable."

"Nee. Cloth is better. It's not so bad to use a wringer. You get used to it."

"It's easier to get used to electricity," he added with a crooked grin.

"Maybe." She stacked the dry clothes in the basket and sat back in her chair. "Jeff, what do you know about leukemia?"

"Not much. I had a cousin who died two years ago from it, but it was the worst kind known. It's hard to believe Katie has it. She doesn't look sick."

"She drags herself though. She used to be spunky, according to her family."

"That's a shame, but they seem optimistic about getting it under control. Honey, when do you think we can talk to your family about us?"

"Not yet. Too much going on and I don't want to get them upset anymore than I have to. You said you wanted to wait at least a year, right?"

"If we can wait that long. I do need to get more schooling first and save some money. Things are tight right now."

"When I come home, I've decided I'll go to the meeting house with you, at least once."

A smile spread across his face. "Good. I think you'll like it. I've met some really nice people there. Very friendly."

"I know. I have Mennonite friends, too. Mostly at the marketplace. They don't bake as gut as we do."

"Sounds a little like bragging, girl," he teased, squeezing her hand.

"Jah, it is. Don't tell. It ain't—I mean, it isn't right for an Amish girl to be proud, but I know gut pie when I taste it, and they don't use enough molasses in their shoo-fly pies."

Jeff laughed and stood up. "Since you're allowed a little conceit, maybe I'll brag a little. I milked a dozen cows. Of course your brother milked two dozen in the same period of time."

It was Belinda's turn to laugh. "Goodness, when you have your own herd, it could take you all morning to milk them. Plus again in the afternoon!"

They laughed and she put his correction of her speech out of her mind. Or tried to.

Jeff rose and stretched. "I guess I'd better go check to see if Leroy wants any more help. I don't want to be in the way here."

"Nee, he appreciates you helping. I heard him tell Aenti Mary just this afternoon."

"I'm glad. I want to have a good relationship with your whole family."

They'll all love you—if you turn Amish." She stood and took his arm as they walked toward the barn. "Are you coming next week-end?"

"I hope to. I don't know about Carrie. I haven't talked to her about it. She tell you she's going on a date with Dan?"

"Nee. Why? He's nothing but trouble."

"I warned her, but you know my sister. She has a mind of her own."

"Oh, jah. Don't we all? Come on, I'll check the tomatoes before I go back."

She dropped his arm and they walked slightly apart, avoiding any physical contact. It wouldn't be a good idea to show any intimacy. There were enough problems in the household without creating further complications.

Chapter Twenty-One
Lancaster County, Pennsylvania

Sunday, Carrie offered to remain at home with Oma while the rest of the family rode over to the church service held at a neighbor's barn. It was the first time Jeff had attended an Amish service. Though he wasn't dressed in their attire, he blended well with his simple style of clothing. Wayne introduced him to several of his friends and he waved over at Belinda once as he took his seat with the other men.

Things seemed so familiar, she could have been in Ohio. Though the faces were different, the service was almost identical to hers at home. The singsong quality of the sermon was a gentle reminder of the pleasant Sundays she'd experienced over the years in her own Amish community. How would it feel to leave all this and worship with the Mennonites? Was Jeff asking too much of her?

After the service, the men moved the benches while the women worked together preparing the tables of food. Mary had made a huge pot of baked beans and Katie had prepared a fruit salad with help from her sister-in-law, Hannah.

Once when they were working together, Katie leaned over and whispered to Belinda. "If you look over by the desserts, the tall girl talking to the old lady is Priscilla."

Belinda glanced over at Katie's competition. "She's not so great," she whispered back. "Is Josiah here?"

"Nee. Thank goodness. I couldn't handle that. I didn't want to come today, but I felt the need to worship. I need God so much right now."

"Always, Katie. But I know what you mean." Belinda put her hand on Katie's arm. She could feel her shaking slightly. "Are you okay?"

"Nee. I'd better sit. I can't eat right now. I'll *kutz* if I do."

"Do you think you should leave? Your family brought two carriages. Maybe your brother should take you home."

"I'll rest a minute. I don't want to cause a fuss. No one knows about…"

"Well, sit down and I'll bring you some water."

She sat on a bench as Belinda went for a glass. Mary looked over and came to her side. "Honey, are you sick?"

"I'll be all right. Belinda's getting me some water." With that, Belinda returned and handed her the glass. She looked over at Mary, who was pale, herself. "Should we get Onkel Leroy? Maybe you should both head home. Jeff could take you home in one of the buggies if the others want to stay."

"Jah, maybe," Mary responded. "First we'll get something to eat. I feel a little faint."

"Oh, goodness," Belinda said as she looked around for Jeff. When she spotted him, she went over and told him what happened. They walked back to the bench where Mary and Katie were resting. Belinda suggested Jeff and she would bring food over for them.

Mary nodded. "Not too much. A little portion of potato salad and a small slice of ham is all."

"Nothing for me, though," Katie said. "I'm way too sick to my stomach. We should leave after Mamm eats a little something."

Jeff went and informed Leroy, who headed over to their side. After some of their neighbors wrapped up dishes with food, Leroy brought their buggy around and they headed for the farm. Though they left a few minutes later, Belinda and Jeff pulled in at the same time with his car.

No sooner had Katie entered the house than she ran for the bathroom and vomited. Mary went swiftly to her side and knelt by the toilet to hold her daughter's head while she wretched. Belinda felt faint herself as she heard the poor girl suffer. So sad.

Jeff came in a few minutes later, somber-faced and concerned. He drew Belinda aside and mentioned he and Carrie would be leaving within the hour. She nodded. "I'm sorry it turned out like this. I was hoping we'd have a gut day."

"It was good until this happened, Belinda. I really liked the service, though I don't understand the German you speak. Even though I took German in school, this was different. I could make out some of the words, but..."

She smiled. "I know. It takes time to learn. That's all I heard in my home growing up. I didn't learn English till I was in school."

"I'm glad the Mennonites don't speak in another language."

Belinda felt her heart drop. It certainly didn't sound as if he would consider turning Amish—even for her. God would work it out. She had too much on her mind now to concern herself with that.

As they prepared to leave, Belinda filled a toot with Snickerdoodles, which she had made earlier in the week. She handed it to Jeff as he placed his sister's overnight case in the trunk. "I put extra cookies in for my daed. It's his favorite kind of cookie. Could you take some over to him when you have a chance?"

"Of course. I'd better do it right away, or there won't be any to take over," he said with a smile.

"I used a large bag, just in case," she said, smiling back. "You can come next week then?"

"I'll give it my best try. The only problem would be school. I have a paper due and it counts as a heavy part of my grade. I'm going to try to work on it a little every night. You know I'll be here if at all possible."

"Jah, I know."

Carrie and Wayne walked out of the house together and went over to the car. Wayne ran his hand along the side of the shiny black fender. "I sure wish I could drive," he said pensively.

"It's not all it's cracked up to be. Between upkeep, insurance, prices at the pump—it costs a lot to run a car."

"Jah, I'm sure, but it's gotta be super fun to speed."

Jeff and Belinda heard his comment as they approached the car.

Jeff slapped Wayne lightly on the arm. "Maybe next time you can take a spin here on your farm."

Wayne grinned and then turned toward Carrie. "Are you coming back with your brudder?"

"Not next week, I'm afraid. Maybe in November. Your grandmother is so sweet. I love taking care of her."

"Jah? You'll be a gut nurse."

"Thank you, Wayne." Carrie stepped forward and gave him a hug. He looked so startled, Belinda nearly broke out laughing. His neck turned pink, then red, then bright scarlet.

After they drove away, Belinda walked slowly back to the house and to the sink of dirty dishes. It would be a long week. She sighed and put a pot of coffee on before tackling the scrapple-crusted frying pan from breakfast. *Help me, God.*

Holmes County, Ohio

Tuesday afternoon, Jeff got out of work an hour early. His classes didn't start until evening, so he headed over to Belinda's parents to give them the cookies she had made and to say hello. When he pulled around back by the barn, he spotted Nellie pouring milk in bowls for the barn cats. She looked over and waved. Then she and her father walked over to the car.

"How's it going?" Jed asked as he reached across for Jeff's hand.

"Good. Thought I'd come by to visit if you have some time."

"Oh, jah. I'm pretty beat up tonight—harvesting time, you know. Gideon's still working, but it gets dark early now. Come on in and have some kaffi with us."

"I have to finish taking care of my cats, Jeff. See you later." Nellie turned back toward the barn as the men went into the kitchen through the back door. Grace was finishing the supper clean up when they arrived. She nodded over at Jeff, but scarcely smiled.

"These are for you. Belinda wanted me to bring them by." He handed over the bag of cookies to Jed, who looked at him with furrowed brow.

"When did she give you these?" he asked.

"Uh, Sunday before I left Pennsylvania."

"You were there this past week-end?" His voice had an edge.

"I went with Carrie. She wanted to help out."

"Mmm. Sit. Grace, put some on a plate." The men took seats and Jed sat back in his chair, pulling at his beard with one hand. "Sohn, we need to talk."

154

Jeff didn't like his tone. It didn't sound friendly.

"Sure. Please, you start."

"I think things are getting out of hand. With you and our dochder."

"Out of hand?"

"Jah. We know you two are gut friends and that's okay, but unless you take on the Amish faith, it ain't going any further. Do you understand?"

"In all due respect, sir, Belinda is a grown woman—"

"She's under my roof. She may look like a grown woman, but she's still innocent and immature."

"She's really quite mature and she has a mind of her own."

"Oh, we know that," added Grace, who had taken a seat between them. The cookies sat untouched.

"I guess I may as well be frank with you," Jeff said haltingly.

"Yah, honesty would be a nice change," Jed said, sober-faced.

"We haven't lied to anyone. In fact, we wanted to talk to you together, but because she had to go help her family…"

"Talk about what?" Jed asked.

"About us. Our relationship. You see, we've fallen in love and we want to get married."

"Oh, dear Jesus," Grace said under her breath. "Just what I've feared."

Jed shook his head. "I like you Jeff. You know that. If you were Amish, we wouldn't even need to have this conversation, but you're not."

"You know I'm going to be a Mennonite," Jeff said.

"I know that, but they ain't Amish people. There's a difference."

"I'd be willing to give up electricity, if it would help."

"You don't understand. It ain't about lights or no lights, buggies or cars, it goes much deeper. For generations, we Amish have stuck together. We are more than a community. We're like one close family. We care about each other; pray for each other; when someone's in need, we're there to help. You see it yourself. Look at Belinda. She wanted to stay home, but she knew she was needed and the right thing to do was to put her own wants away and lend a hand. She could be there another year or even two. That's what a gut Amish girl does."

Jeff looked down at the table. The coffee no longer steamed. What did it matter? What did anything matter? "I thought we could handle our differences. You can't believe how much I care for your daughter."

"I don't doubt your love for her—or hers for you. But if you made her leave the Amish life, someday she'd regret it and then what would she feel for you? She'd probably be shunned."

"Even though we're so close in our beliefs?"

"I'm afraid so. I'd have to talk to the Bishop, but I see no point now."

"What if I became Amish then?"

"It ain't something you can just turn off and on. Amish is more than the odd clothes and riding in buggies. It's a way of living. A way of thinking. You can't put it on like a jacket."

"I know that. But maybe if you teach me what you believe in, I can believe the same way. Perhaps I already do and just don't realize it."

"Jeff, Jeff. Listen to your foolish talk. I know it's hard to give someone up whom you love. But for Belinda's sake, can't you see what this would do to her? To her whole family? Ain't that a bit selfish of you?"

Jeff shook his head over and over. "I'm not selfish. I just love Belinda so much and I know she feels the same way toward me. We've talked about marriage."

"I feel like you've betrayed me. You went behind my back and I'm not happy about that. Belinda is a confused young woman. Look at all she's put us through, but I think I know her better than you do. In time, she'll get over you. I'm sorry to be so blunt. I don't want to hurt you, but I have to think of what's best for my dochder. In the long run, it would be better if she married an Amish man. Someday she'll understand."

"I don't know what to say.

"For one thing, I want you to promise you won't go running off to Pennsylvania every week to see her."

"Sir, I can't promise that."

Jed stared over at Jeff, his mouth agape. "Then we have nothing further to say to each other." He rose and left the room, with his shoulders slumped and his head down.

Jeff sat there and stared straight ahead. Then he was aware of Grace rising from the table. He looked up at her and her eyes had turned to stone. No words were spoken, but she removed the plate of cookies and turned her back.

He left as if in a trance. His eyes focused on the car, everything else was a blur. He thought he heard Nellie call out to him, but he went straight to his car and turned on the engine. After focusing on the drive, he slowly moved his vehicle toward the road. What should he say to Belinda when he called? What was their future? How could he have botched things up so badly? *Oh, God, help me.*

Chapter Twenty-Two
Lancaster County, Pennsylvania

Belinda lay across her bed, exhausted from her day caring for Oma. Jeff would soon be calling—the highlight of her day.

Katie had returned from the doctor's office discouraged. She had no appetite and the medication still affected her, causing not only nausea, but dizziness as well. After eating only half a bowl of potato soup, she excused herself and went to bed around six. Belinda noticed her coloring was poor and her energy level seemed to be decreasing each day.

Thankfully, Mary was gradually improving and was able to take over more of the cooking, though she still spent a good part of each afternoon resting.

The atmosphere in the home was depressing. It took all she had for Belinda to maintain a pleasant demeanor for those around her. Oma, too, had become more dependent and lethargic, sleeping between her therapy sessions and meal times.

Jeff seemed restrained the last time they spoke, and since she had been preoccupied herself, she waited with anticipation for this evening's call. It was already later than usual. Perhaps she'd call him, though he'd been faithful about initiating their calls. She could wait a bit longer. Closing her eyes, she allowed sleep to overtake her.

The ring of her cell phone startled her out of her slumber. When she heard his voice, her body relaxed.

"I'm sorry I'm late calling, Belinda. I had to stay after class to get some information from the teacher. Were you sleeping?"

"Just dozing a little, but I've been anxious to hear from you."

"How's everything going in Pennsylvania?"

"Same. Dismal as always. I wish I were home. Oh, well, in two days I'll be seeing you."

"Oh, honey, I can't make it this week-end."

"Nee? No explanation?"

"I may as well tell you. I've been holding off. I guess I just wanted to mull things over before I told you what happened at your parents' home two nights ago."

"Something happened? Is everyone okay?"

"They're fine. It's about us. I didn't realize your parents didn't know I went to see you last week-end."

"So?"

"So, they weren't real happy about it. In fact, your father has forbidden me to go see you."

"Forbidden! He can't do that!"

"He thinks he can, and maybe since you're still at home, he's right. Belinda, I told him we intend to marry."

"Good grief. Did you have to?"

"I felt it was necessary. I didn't want him to think I was just trying to take advantage of a pretty girl."

"He likes you, Jeff. He told me himself. Did you explain about my not being baptized yet and that we'd be black-car Mennonites?"

"He knows all that, but he thinks you'd be banned if you married outside the Amish faith. Maybe you would. I don't know. Maybe I'm asking too much of you—"

"Jeff, stop! I want to marry you! I've never wanted anything so much in my life. Okay, then, I'll yank over! I don't care. He can't ruin my life like this!"

"Honey, slow down. There's got to be a better way. Let me look into the Amish beliefs more. After all, I wouldn't be losing my family like you would. I can't do that to you. I know how much everyone means to you."

"Not anymore. Not if they're going to treat me like this. Not to see you? That's ridiculous! It's not like we're doing anything bad. I won't give up my whole future just because he's so old-fashioned."

"It's deeper than that. Look, honey, I'm going to be super busy this week-end anyway studying and Carrie's busy, so let's sit on this another week before you say or do anything irreversible. Okay?"

Belinda breathed slowly and closed her eyes. "Jeff, you still want to marry me, don't you?"

"Of course I do. We *will* be married someday, but we need to do it right. Let's take the time to figure it all out. You know I love you with all my heart."

She smiled into the phone. "You're right. You always are. Okay, I'll slow down and pray about it and as long as I know you haven't changed your mind about me, I can deal with the bumps along the road."

"That's the right attitude. We have to do things in a Godly way, Belinda, or nothing will be right. I have a brutal headache, honey, so I need to get to bed. I'll call you tomorrow night and we'll spend more time talking."

"I'm sorry about your headache. Too much stress?"

"Probably, but I'll be fine with a good night's sleep. Good night, honey."

"*Gut nacht*, Jeff."

Belinda hung up and lay on her back, staring at the ceiling. A small cobweb caught her attention and she watched it shift, casting a frail shadow on the wall. Like her life. Shifting. Fragile. Would things really rectify themselves? Could their two worlds ever come together to

160

allow them the future they so desired? *Oh, Lord, I pray we can one day be married. Please help us find the right course to take. I've learned so much these last few months, but there is so much more I need to understand. I know you want what's best for your children, but it seems there are always obstacles along the path. Give me patience and love and wisdom.*

Belinda turned down the lamp and closed her eyes again. There was the semblance of peace in her spirit. She released all her fears and turmoil to her Creator. Her burdens may be heavy, but His yoke was strong.

The next night, Josiah figured he'd waited enough time for Katie to think things through. He couldn't wait another day to see her. Surely she had calmed down enough to look at events through rational eyes. He looked at the clock again. Katie should be done with her supper by now. She should have time to speak with him in private.

After all the hours he'd spent harvesting with his brothers, he finally had the time to go to Katie and mend their broken relationship. Time had not healed his pain. Not at all. He missed her with all his being. Why had she assumed the worst when she saw Priscilla at his home? His home. It was meant to be *their* home. Surely Katie hadn't meant it when she called it a shack. She'd been so excited earlier. He should have been more understanding when he paid visits to her home. Of course, she couldn't give him her undivided attention. It was immature to expect that. The sweet girl was doing everything she could to help her aged grandmother and take some of the burden off her own mother, who had been so ill herself. He felt shame when he thought about his reaction to her lack of time for him. If only he could live it over.

He dampened his comb and raked through his hair, placing the straw hat on top before heading toward his open buggy. After harnessing his horse, he made his way over to her farmhouse. As he pulled in, he could see Wayne and Leroy wiping down some of their equipment. They turned and waved as he drew closer. Katie was nowhere to be seen.

"Greetings," he said with a nervous smile. "I see you have your harvest in. Gut crop this year?"

"Jah, the best in years," Leroy said. "How's your place coming along?"

"Pretty gut. Kind of at a standstill for now. Not much incentive."

Wayne linked his hands in his suspenders and looked down at the ground.

"Is Katie around?" Josiah asked.

"I don't know what she's up to," Leroy said. "Go in the back. It's open."

Josiah nodded, tipped his hat and made his way to the back porch. He heard women's voices as he reached the screen door and knocked on the trim. Belinda came to the door and opened it. She let out a short gasp before saying hello. Then instead of inviting him in, she stood motionless.

"Can I come in?"

"Oh, jah. Come on. Katie's lying down."

"Is she sick?"

"She's tired, is all."

"Can I wait for her?" He looked over at Mary and smiled. "Hallo, Mrs. Zook. Are you all better now?"

"Pretty gut, I guess. Katie may not be down for awhile."

He stood, hat in hand, and looked from her to Belinda. "It's real important that I see her. I can wait outside if you want."

162

"It may be a long wait," Mary added. She wrapped her arms around her waist and stared at him.

"It's real important. Could you just tell her I'm here? I'd appreciate it."

The women exchanged glances. Then Mary nodded at Belinda. "You can go tell her, but don't wake her up if she's sleeping. She had a bad night."

"You can sit and wait, I guess," Mary said as she went over to the stove and wiped down the burners. She kept her back to him.

Belinda walked over to the staircase and ascended the steps.

"Katie, can I come in?" Belinda asked softly as she turned the knob and peeked in. Katie was reading in bed and looked up in surprise.

"Sure. Is something wrong?"

"You have a visitor. Josiah."

Katie closed the book and stared straight ahead. "Tell him I'm asleep."

"Katie, I don't want to lie, and besides, he seems determined to see you."

"I have nothing to say to him. Make that plain."

"Are you sure this is what you really want? Maybe he came to apologize. Don't be too quick to close all doors."

She looked over at Belinda. "I can't deal with anything more in my life right now. I can't explain it. I'm just living a day at a time now. I can't handle anything more complicated. Please make up an excuse."

Belinda took a step back into the hall. "Okay. Whatever you want."

When she went back into the kitchen, it was silent. Mary scrubbed and re-scrubbed the same burner while

Josiah sat looking out the window. When he heard her return, he stood up.

"She's not able to come down now. She said you should go home. And...not...come back. I'm sorry."

He nodded and his jaw tightened. "Here, I was afraid this would happen, so I wrote her a letter. Please see she gets it."

Belinda reached over and took the sealed envelope from his hand. "I'll give it to her."

"Danki." He walked toward the door and said good-by. Mary nodded as he left. Once they heard his buggy grind over the coarse pebbles, Mary let out a long breath. "I hope Katie ain't being foolish. He was a gut man, I thought."

"I understand her not wanting to see him right now. With everything she's dealing with, I guess it would be too much to have false hopes and all."

"Jah, probably. Poor girl. She was so happy a few months ago and now look at her. Why don't you take his letter up anyway? She don't have to read it right away, but when it's the right time, maybe it will make a difference."

Belinda went up and knocked again. "Come in," Katie said. She was just lying there, the book by her side. Her eyes were red and puffy and there were several rumpled tissues on her quilt.

"He left, but he wanted you to have this." Belinda placed the letter next to Katie's pillow.

"I can't read it now. Maybe later. Or maybe I'll just rip it up. It won't make any difference what he wrote."

"Katie, give him a chance to explain. There may be a very logical explanation for everything that happened."

"Oh, it's logical all right. He wanted a girlfriend. I was busy caring for my sick grossmammi and he was upset, poor baby. Along comes a pretty girl with a bad reputation, and boom. We're done. End of explanation."

"You could be all wrong, Katie. I'd read the letter if I were you."

"We'll see. I'm going to bed now. Do you need me for anything first?"

"Nee, everything is under control. Your mamm is doing ever so much better, thank God."

"Jah, at least something is going gut. Danki for covering for me."

"It's okay, but someday, you'll have to see him, whether you want to or not. After all, you're in the same community. You'll have to accept it."

"When I have to, I will. Right now, I don't have to do anything I don't want to."

Belinda shook her head. "I hope you have a gut sleep for a change."

"Jah, me, too. I'll be in a better mood tomorrow, I'm sure. I'm sorry things are the way they are. I know you'd rather be in Ohio with your family."

"Someday, everything will straighten out, I'm sure. For you, too, Katie. All in God's timing."

"Yah, and His timing is not ours. I have to remind myself of that all the time. I just want to be well again and not have this scary thing hanging over me."

Belinda reached over and touched Katie's cheek. "You're very brave. I really admire you, Kate."

"Danki." Katie covered Belinda's hand with her own and choked back tears.

After Belinda left, Katie ran her hand under the seal and removed the sheet of paper with Josiah's handwriting. She couldn't feel any worse than she did, so what did it matter what the letter contained?

Chapter Twenty-Three
Holmes County, Ohio

Saturday, Jeff spent the entire day studying and working on a paper, which was due on Monday. It would have been difficult to travel to Pennsylvania, though if her parents hadn't requested, no—*insisted,* that he stay away from Belinda, he would have made the trip. It was difficult to be so far from the woman he loved.

His mother, Linda, knocked on his bedroom door around seven in the evening and suggested he break for supper. "Your father's cooking ribs on the grill. You have to stop long enough to re-fuel."

"I'll be down. Just give me ten more minutes and then I'll quit for the night."

When he came down, Carrie was opening the front door for Dan, who was taking her to a restaurant in town for dinner. He was wearing a sport jacket with a white cotton turtleneck. Carrie wore a knee-high silk dress, revealing too much skin—as far as Jeff was concerned. Not like advertising your product, he thought, fuming at her lack of modesty.

The men greeted each other coolly, and then his sister and Dan left and Jeff joined his parents in the kitchen.

His father, Bob, looked up as he came in the room. "You must be weary of studying, son. You've been at it all day."

"Yeah, I've done all I can for one day. I'll do more after church tomorrow."

"Going with your friend to the Mennonite place?"

"Right. You should come with us some Sunday," Jeff suggested.

"No, I'm happy where we go. Good preaching, plus we have a lot of friends there."

Linda brought over a tossed salad. "The tomatoes are good this year. So juicy."

They took their seats and Bob said grace, They ate silently, and when they were done with the main course, they sat together over coffee.

"I've been meaning to talk to you about something, Jeff," his father began. "Your mother and I have been discussing your future and we're willing to pay your full tuition if you transfer at the end of the year to a four-year college and get your degree. How does that sound?"

"That's great of you guys to offer, but it's working all right the way it is. Even with an associate's degree, I think I'll have enough knowledge to run my own business."

His father leaned back and folded his arms. "A bachelor's degree means more in the outside world, Jeff, and maybe you'll decide to go into another field of work. It would give you the resume you'd need. I was thinking about Oberlin or even Bucknell in Pennsylvania where my brother went. Good schools. This is the time, while you're single and free to do what you please."

Jeff poured a second cup of coffee and stirred in some cream. He studied the creamy liquid before answering. "I don't want to stay single too much longer."

His mother let out a laugh. "Well, I didn't know you'd found the lucky woman yet."

"I have."

Her smile turned to a frown. "Really? Who on earth are you talking about?"

"Belinda."

167

Her parents exchanged glances. Then his father cleared his throat. "I didn't think it was serious. For heaven's sake, Jeff, she's Amish. You know she won't leave her family to marry an outsider."

"Now that I'm going to be a Mennonite, the gap has lessened."

"That's another issue we should discuss. The Mennonites are an extremist group and—"

"You can't be serious! Extremists? They are totally laid back and peace-loving people. They have all the right values and they—"

"Maybe I used the wrong word, but look how they dress. You'd think it was 1940 the way they wear their hair and the women wear their dresses. Do you want to be stared and maybe laughed at?"

"I can't believe you're talking like this. Just because the women want to dress modestly, you think they're mocked?"

"Well, I would never mock anyone, but you know what I mean."

"No, Dad, I don't. And I'd even consider going Amish if that's the only way I can marry Belinda."

"Oh, Jeff," his mother said. "You're not thinking rationally. You may have a crush on this girl, but—"

"It's not a crush. I'm totally, one hundred percent in love with her and she feels the same about me."

His father leaned forward. "If that's the case, let her become a Presbyterian. Why should you be the one to change your whole life?"

"First off, I wouldn't lose my family if I changed to Amish, whereas, she'd be giving up everything."

"Well, I can't imagine you'd be invited to any of our family affairs if you ended up with a funny beard and black suspenders holding up your pants," his mother remarked, brows puckered.

"Son, calm down," his father said as he sat back. "Let's try to see this through the proper lens. I know this Belinda girl is attractive and I'm sure the fact that she's Amish even adds to her appeal in some distorted way, but she probably hasn't even graduated high school."

"They don't go after eighth grade," Jeff inserted.

"Just what I mean. The girl is uneducated. How would she feel around your friends?"

"She and Carrie are close friends."

His mother laid a hand over his. "Just friends, though. That's what you should be. Just a friend. There's nothing wrong with that, but to think you'd marry her? Jeff, where is your brain?"

Jeff rose from the table and collected several soiled plates and headed for the sink. "I guess this conversation is going no where. I'm going back to my studies. Thanks for dinner."

"I'm sorry you're being so difficult to talk to," his father remarked, glaring up at his son. "This isn't the end of the discussion."

"Whatever. I'm sorry, but I have my own life to live. I feel God is leading me in my decisions."

"God. God. I suppose you hear him talk to you now." His father's jaw tightened.

"You'll never understand. Excuse me." Jeff left the room abruptly and headed for his room. Things were not going as planned. Would the whole world be against them? All they wanted was to marry and love each other. Was that such a terrible thing?

Lancaster County, Pennsylvania

Katie slipped the three-page folded letter out of the envelope and held it close to her chest before reading it. Her heart pounded as she saw his irregular writing. She smiled when she remembered trying to read his grocery list one time and how she teased him when she purchased Band-Aids instead of bananas, all because of his sloppy script. She began to read.

> *Dear Katie,*
>
> *Since I haven't been able to talk to you in person I thought I'd better write to you. I'm sorry you are never available when I come by, but I hope you will not tear this up before reading it.*
>
> *First of all, I am very, very sorry for any pain I've caused you. I would never hurt you on purpose. You must know that. When you came by and Priscilla showed up, I was just as surprised as you were. Okay, I admit it wasn't the first time, but we never did anything immoral. You have to believe me, Katie. I love you and always will, and I would never do anything to change that. Priscilla is pushy and I didn't know how to tell her to stop coming by, but I knew I'd have to somehow make it clear to her that it was not a good idea. I've seen her since, once at a Sing. I went on purpose, because I wanted to tell her in a group setting to lay off. I thought it would be easier with people around. She laughed when I told her not to stop by again and she said she wasn't planning to, because I was boring and not that hot. Never thought I'd like to hear words like that, but in this case I was glad. Honest.*

Now, what can we do about this? I think if you will let me see you in person, we can work it all out. I know you have been under a lot of strain with your mother being sick and all and trying to help with your grandmother. I should have been more understanding, and I guess I acted like a jerk to want more alone time with you. It was selfish and I'm sorry.

What's in our future? Well, I hope with all my heart that you will be my wife (any time you say) and we can live happily ever after with our children, born from our love, and our families near-by. You are a wonderful person and I'd consider it a real honor if you'd come back to me and accept my proposal. (again)

I will not bother you for a little while since I want you to have time to think about everything I've said. But I'm going to come by on November 14th to talk to you. Please be there. You may remember, that was the day we hoped to be married, so I think it's a good day to talk.

Love always and forever,
Josiah

Katie read it again. And once more. He certainly sounded sincere. Perhaps she had jumped to the wrong conclusions. Priscilla was known to be forward. He even explained the Sing he attended. It kind of made sense.

Katie reached for tissues and wiped her eyes.

But what if she wasn't able to bear children? When things were going well between them, she and Josiah had talked about having a big family. His eyes lit up when he talked about teaching his boys how to hunt and fish. And he'd hugged Katie once and said he wanted all his daughters to look just like her. Now, there was a strong possibility she would never be able to bear children. Ever.

She reached for more tissues and blew her nose. *Oh, why Lord? Where did this horrible illness come from?* She wasn't even sure if the medication was working. They wouldn't know for a while. The nausea was a constant reminder of the poison in her body. What if it didn't work at all? She could die in the next year or so. It wouldn't be fair to get back together again with Josiah, only to have them separated through her untimely death. And even if she was in remittance some day, was it fair to marry a man knowing you might not be able to carry his boppli?

Josiah. She still loved him with her whole heart. She had never really stopped caring. She had been lying to herself—out of pain and anger. It made it easier, perhaps to pretend it no longer mattered. But oh, it did. It so mattered. The emptiness she felt after their break-up was as awful, in its way, as the pain of knowing she had leukemia. Different, but just as great an ache to her whole being. It would be so easy to ask him back in her life. It would never be the same, though. She'd have to watch him as he sorrowed after his own flesh and blood children. Or maybe watch her deteriorate and die before his eyes. How would that be fair?

When he stops by in November, I won't see him. It would only make it more difficult. For his sake, I will remain out of his life. He'll get over me eventually, perhaps sooner than I'd like, and he'll find another Amish woman—complete—who will be his soul-mate and raise his family.

The tears wouldn't stop and she burrowed her face in her pillow to smother her cries. She would not be a burden to her family. Maybe she and Becky could teach together and she'd enjoy, whatever time she had left with her nieces and nephews, and she could be a comfort to Oma and her parents. Marriage wasn't the only answer for her. Doing God's will—that was the most important thing in her life. Now and always. As she turned to God in prayer, her sobs subsided, and Katie looked to her future with new hope.

Chapter Twenty-Four
Holmes County, Ohio

Carrie wrapped her creamy lace shawl around her shoulders as she and Dan walked from the car to the restaurant. This time there were no friends waiting for them. They were led to a small round table for two, which was a distance from the dance floor. Lighting was low with soft music surrounding them as they sat and perused the overly large menus. A waiter in black slacks and vest came over and told them the specials. Then a younger man poured ice water in their goblets and asked about a drink order. Dan ordered a bottle of champagne and continued to study his menu.

"So what does the lady desire tonight?" he said, glancing over at Carrie, who was concentrating on her choices.

"Goodness, there's so much to choose from. Maybe the *poulet francais*. I like chicken."

"What about the rack of lamb?"

"Too much food."

"By the time you take away the bones, there's not a lot of meat left, but it's tasty. I've had it here before."

After considerable discussion, they both ordered the chicken and the waiter returned with two tulip glasses and poured a small amount of champagne in each glass.

"I've never had champagne," Carrie remarked as she held the glass up to their candle and watched the bubbles cluster to the top. "Hope I like it."

"You will. Guaranteed. So," he added, as he lifted his glass towards hers, "to us. To our future together." They each sipped and then set the glasses back on the table.

"You think we have a future together?" Carrie asked, tilting her head to one side.

"I know it."

She laughed. "I think I have some say in it, don't you?"

"Honey," he said in a low voice, "you and I are made for each other. I knew it the first time I met you."

"Really? Funny, you went through four of my friends before you even asked me out."

"I always save the best for last."

"You are a very conceited man, you know. What makes you think this is it? The big one? We've only had one real date before tonight."

"I don't usually feel this way, Carrie. You make my heart dance."

"Corny."

"What did you say?" He looked over and grinned. "I guess that's one reason I like you. You say what you think."

"Don't you?"

"Depends upon what I'm thinking. Right now, while we wait for our dinners, the music is playing some of my favorite dance music. Will you join me?" He started to rise and extended his hand to her at the same time.

"I guess."

They danced for several minutes to slow swing music. He was a good dancer, all right. Too good. Too smooth. Too tempting. She'd have to avoid drinking any more champagne. She felt his lips graze the side of her neck. "Please, don't do that." He withdrew, but made it plain he wasn't pleased with her reaction. Her resistance to this handsome man was dropping like hail on a pavement. Not good. Probably her brother was right to warn her. Dan was smooth as a dancer, a talker, a boyfriend. Goodness, it's only a date. Certainly she was safe.

They finally returned to their table and ate their meal. Service was efficient, but relaxed. Before she realized it, they'd been there over three hours.

"I'd better get home, Dan. I'm leaving early tomorrow for school. A friend is having a bridal shower and I promised to help set up."

"It's early. It's not even midnight. Why don't you come back to my place? My folks are away for the weekend. We can sit and talk in private."

"That's not such a hot idea."

"Am I a temptation to you, Carrie?" His smile danced across his gorgeous face and he squeezed her hand and rubbed a thumb over her wrist. She withdrew her hand, a feeling of insecurity sweeping through her.

"No, I'm just tired. Come on, the check's been paid, hasn't it?"

"A long time ago. Okay, I can take a hint." He pushed back his chair and came around to her side. She expected him to pull her chair back and help her up, but he just stood and waited for her to rise.

On the way back to her place, he barely spoke a word and when he got to her drive, he leaned over and pushed the car door open from the inside. She was surprised at how annoyed that made her. Her father still insisted on opening doors for his women and his manners made this young man look downright insolent. Well, she wouldn't forget her own conduct. She thanked him for a nice meal as she shifted her body to make an exit. He nodded and gave her a half smile.

"I'll call you."

"Right." She let the door slam a trifle too loudly and turned toward the path to the front door without looking back to wave.

As she prepared for bed, she thought about the whole evening. It was obvious that he thought he could seduce her with a meal and a drink and clever conversation, but she had passed the test. She did not fall for his game and though she admitted he had momentarily been a temptation, she had held fast to her morals. She thanked God for giving her the strength she needed to avoid his advances and made the decision to never go out with him again or even be alone with him or any other man like him. Jeff was right about him. Maybe she'd attend church with her brother and find a nice guy. A strong Christian man, who had something on his mind besides that three-letter word!

Carrie slept like a babe. Her first eight-hour sleep in two months. Nothing like the right decision to give one peace.

Lancaster County, Pennsylvania

Becky dropped onto the desk chair after the last student left for the weekend. It had been a grueling day. With the crisp days of autumn upon them, the children were restless in class, wanting instead to be out playing ball or jumping in the colorful piles of leaves. Without her assistant, who had been out two weeks with the flu, she was left with all the work on her own shoulders. Though she loved teaching, she found it draining. It was much more fun when Katie taught alongside her. They had worked well together. Katie. She needed to get by to see her. The last she heard, Katie was definitely through with Josiah. It had come as such a surprise to everyone.

She glanced at her watch. She should stop by and see her friend. The last church day, she hadn't made it due to a difficult monthly. In fact, it had been nearly a month since she'd connected with her best friend.

Becky made sure everything was tidy before she took her open buggy and headed to the Zook's. When she arrived, she spotted Wayne, who was mulching the family vegetable garden. Funny, usually Katie liked to prepare the beds for winter.

Wayne looked up and waved. Then he dropped his shovel against the wheelbarrow and headed her way. She felt her heart take a leap.

"Hey, Beck. What's new?"

"Not much. The kids drove me a bit crazy this week, but other than that, my life's pretty much same ole, same ole. What about you?"

"Ach. Boring, kind of. Are you here to see Katie?"

"Jah, it's been a while. Is she in the house?"

"Probably lying down."

"In the middle of the afternoon?"

He looked down at the ground and cleared his throat. "Sometimes she gets tired."

"Anything new with Josiah?"

"You'd better ask her. I try to stay out of that stuff. Here, I'll take care of your horse. Go on in. Belinda baked brownies this morning."

"Gut timing on my part," she said grinning. "Are you gonna come in and have one, too?"

"Oh, jah. I can smell them from here."

Becky went and knocked at the back door. Belinda opened it and invited her in. Katie was nowhere in sight. After saying hello to everyone, Becky made her way to Katie's room. The door was closed. She knocked softly in case Katie was sleeping.

"Come in," Katie said in a low voice.

When she saw her best friend, lying against her pillow, her face gaunt and expressionless, it was all she could do not to gasp. What had happened to make her look so sickly? "Katie, what's wrong? Is it because of Josiah?"

Katie pushed herself to a sitting position, propping an extra pillow behind her back. She raised the wick on the lamp and tried to smile. "Nee, I just don't feel so gut today."

"You should see a doctor. Maybe you're sick."

"Becky, I am sick. Real sick. I haven't told many people and I don't want you to tell anyone else, but I have leukemia."

Becky clasped her hand to her mouth, shock emanating from every pore. "Nee, it can't be! Oh, Katie." She put her head in her hands and openly cried for her dear friend.

"Becky, it's not that bad. I'm probably not going to die right away. In fact, I'm on medication and they hope it will stop the progress of the disease and even make me feel better. Please don't cry like this." She moved to the side of the bed and took Becky in her arms.

"I can't believe this is happening. You're too young for something so serious."

"Well, jah, I think so, too, but it happens."

"Will you lose your hair?"

"I hope not. I'm on oral drugs. They aren't as strong as radiation."

"You won't need radiation?"

"At this point they think oral medicine will work. Time will tell."

"Have you told Josiah?"

Katie breathed out a long slow breath. "Nee, and I don't plan to."

"He'd be back if he knew."

"Becky, I don't want him back out of pity."

"But he loves you. I know he does."

Katie removed her crushed kapp and let her hair fall to her waist. Then she laid back against the pillow. "I haven't seen him since we broke up. But he's stopped by a couple times. Last time, when I wouldn't see him, he left a letter for me. I'll let you read it." She rolled over, reached into the drawer of her bedside table and handed Becky the envelope.

Becky, now in control, moved closer to the window for light, and read it over. When she was finished, she placed it back in the envelope and handed it to Katie.

"What do you think?" Katie asked her friend.

"I think he's still madly in love with you and you ain't being fair to him if you don't tell him about your illness. He'd want to be here for you."

"Becky, I may not be able to have boppli."

"So?"

"So, what Amish man wants a wife who can't have children?"

"Maybe you should ask Josiah. Why should you take it upon yourself to decide for him? You could use his support at this time, right?"

"Of course, but it's not fair to put him in that spot. Knowing him, he'd marry me out of obligation. I can't stand that thought."

"And what if you're wrong and you both still love each other and yet because of your stubbornness, you never get together? Who is that fair to?"

"I don't know. You make it hard to think straight. You read his letter. He's planning to come by in the middle of November. I don't want to see him."

"Oh, Katie, have you prayed about this?"

"Jah, but I ain't heard a strong answer, one way or the other. I'm sick of lying here. I think I'll go downstairs now. Why don't you stay for tea?"

"If you include one of Belinda's brownies, it's a deal."

They went down together. Becky watched Katie as she held on to the railing and walked with effort down the staircase. Her heart was sorely in pain for her dear friend.

Belinda helped Oma into her wheelchair and moved her into the kitchen to join the others for a snack. Leroy came in for tea and a brownie. Wayne sat down across from Becky, placed three large brownies on his plate and then passed the platter to his sister.

"Haven't seen you lately, Becky," Mary stated as she poured a cup of tea for her mother.

"Nee, I've been busy teaching. My helper has been sick. By the time I'm done teaching, I just want to go home and collapse."

Mary nodded. "I know that feeling. How's your family?"

"Gut. Busy. We had a great harvest this year."

Leroy nodded. "It was a gut year for us farmers, that's for certain. I hope you can come by and keep Katie company more often. I think she gets bored sometimes."

"Nee, Daed, I'm not bored. Just tired is all."

He looked down at his cup and stirred it with a spoon. "I guess Katie told you."

"Jah. I was ever so surprised."

"We all were, but she's doing better, ain't you, Katie?" he asked, looking over at her frail body. His suffering for his beloved daughter was apparent in his grieving eyes.

"I think so, Daed. I think the medicine is working. I'll know more in a month or two when they test my blood again."

Mary wiped her eyes. "Can you stay for supper, Becky? It would be gut for all of us to have company."

"Danki. I'd have to go home to tell my family first, or they'd worry, I'm afraid."

"I can ride over and tell them," Wayne offered. "You stay with my schwester."

"That's nice of you, Wayne. Okay."

Oma sipped at her tea and then asked about the number of students Becky took care of.

"We have twenty-four this year. Quite a handful."

"Hey, we used to handle that many in our sleep," Katie said, smiling at her friend.

"Oh, you're right there. I'd love to have you back when you're feeling better, but I know—"

"I might just do that—when I'm feeling stronger. Now that I'm not getting married…"

The room became silent. Then Wayne stuffed the last piece of brownie in his mouth and told them he would head over to Becky's and be home within a few minutes. He tripped out the door and it closed behind him.

Oma bent her arm and rested her head on her fist. "I guess I'll go back to my room now, Belinda, if you don't mind."

"Mamm, it's gut for you to be up and around," Mary said, a slight frown crossing her face.

"I'm too tired, honey. I'll just rest a while."

Belinda rose to help her back to her room.

"I can take her in, Belinda. You've been doing all the work around here today. You need a break."

"Then I'll go check the towels on the line."

Soon it was just Becky and Katie at the table. "You look better when you're up, Katie. You feel okay?"

"Still nauseated. It leaves me with no appetite. I've lost more weight."

"I can see. Everything hangs loose on you. Do you want me to take in your dresses for you?"

"Danki, but Mamm likes to sew. I'll give her the job, or even do it myself. I've accomplished nothing lately. I feel like a total drag on everyone."

"I'm sure they don't see it that way. Oh, Katie, I'm sorry I didn't come sooner. If I'd only known."

"It's okay, really. I needed to work through this whole thing. It was so scary. It took a lot of prayer and thought to get to the place where I've accepted it. No matter how it all ends."

"You are so courageous. I know I couldn't handle news like that as well as you have."

"You would if you had to. It's amazing how God gives us the strength to deal with things like this. I never would have thought it possible to accept it like I have. It's God, Beck, not me."

Becky leaned over and held her friend. "Well, I'm glad I'm able to be standing with you through this. You're going to be well again. I just know it."

After supper, Katie went upstairs early. Wayne walked out with Becky to help with her buggy. "I'm glad you know, Becky. Katie hasn't wanted us to tell anyone outside the family and people are asking me stuff like where is she and what's new. It gets hard to answer sometimes."

Becky patted her horse's head and kept her eyes on the horse, but her thoughts were for Wayne. "I'm sorry for you too, Wayne. I know it must be hard on you."

"Jah, it is. Real hard. I love teasing my schwester, but, well, you know."

Becky nodded. "I know you two have always been real close. I think she's going to get through this real gut, though. Better than we think."

"I hope you're right. I don't know how my mamm could handle things if ..."

Becky turned and touched his arm. "It's not going to end that way. She's young and strong and with the new medication and treatment they have, she'll get over this part."

He looked into her eyes. "You believe that, don't you?"

She nodded. "With all my heart."

He gave her a faint smile. "Danki. That helps."

"I'll come by in a couple days to check on her. Maybe we can take her in the buggy for a drive. The trees are so pretty now."

"Jah, gut idea. Next time, we'll do that. She's always liked autumn."

As Becky pulled away, she turned to wave. Wayne was standing, arms folded, watching her. He had a pleasant expression. The first time she'd seen something close to a smile all day. *Lord, help Wayne deal with this, too.*

Her faithful horse trotted merrily on his way, oblivious to the trials of his mistres

Chapter Twenty-Five
Holmes County, Ohio

Jeff shoved his textbooks to the side of his desk and rested his head on his hands. He hadn't done as well on his last paper as he expected. Probably due to his long hours at work. There were several big jobs, which had to be done before the cold weather set in. Planting trees and protecting fragile shrubbery were high priority. It was nice to earn some extra money, but it played havoc on his studies.

He could still hear Belinda's sobs from the night before after telling her about his conversation with his family. It might get even harder when she returned. Her access to a phone would be limited, if not impossible. She probably would feel guilty to use the one he had bought for her. Then what? Would they have to resort to sneaking around behind people's backs? Could they do something dishonorable like that? What choice would they have with both families against them being together? What was so terrible about them wanting to marry?

Jeff prayed for help. He travailed for over an hour. Sometimes he paced the floor. Sometimes he lay prostrate on his bed and once he spread himself on the rug. The pain was real. He'd never been in love like this. Not even close. His love even made him realize he could give Belinda up, if he believed it would be better for her without him. Trouble was, he didn't believe that. Not for

185

an instant. If he had to, he'd become an Amish man, give up his dreams of owning his own business, and settle for working the land for survival. He'd be satisfied with that, as long as he had Belinda at his side.

He finally made the decision to at least look into the Amish lifestyle with the prospects of changing his religion. But who would teach him the ways? Maybe if he hadn't messed up with Jed, he would have guided him through the Ausbund, but not now. That wasn't an option. He remembered his Mennonite friend, Randy Davidson, spoke once about knowing an Amish man real well. He had worked with him a few times on construction jobs. He'd go check with Randy tomorrow and see if he could work it so they could meet. Better not to mention his idea to Belinda yet, or anyone else. If he couldn't make the transition to the Amish life, there was no reason to raise false hopes. What on earth would his parents think if he went to that extreme?

Jeff was drained after his encounter with God, but he also felt real hope. He showered and went out for a drive. It was still light out, though every day it darkened earlier. He drove through one of his favorite areas where the distant hills were still colorful. The trees had peaked already and now the breezes brought down cascades of leaves, creating a layer of crisp color across the road. He'd miss driving if he changed over. He'd miss a lot of things. Would he give up schooling immediately? He knew the Amish frowned upon getting too much education, but that was with their own people. It was probably different if you joined the Amish after you went to college. Maybe they'd even allow him to finish. So many unanswered questions.

"Oh, Belinda, look what you've done to me. My world is upside down." He couldn't wait to hear her voice again, but she'd be way too busy now. What a trouper. Never complained about the burden of work she'd taken on. How many girls would be willing to give up their lives to help others? Maybe Carrie would, but he couldn't think of anyone else he knew who was that unselfish. He considered himself a fortunate man to have the love of such a wonderful woman.

After driving for nearly an hour, the brilliant sunset made it difficult to drive, so he headed back to his house. His parents were reading in the living room and greeted him, but after a few insignificant comments, they returned to their books and he foraged in the kitchen for food. There were always leftovers. He made himself a cold pork sandwich and returned to his books—renewed in spirit and body. Only two more hours before he'd hear Belinda's voice.

Lancaster County, Pennsylvania

While Mary sat with her mother and the men tended to the animals, Katie and Belinda sat near the kero lamps sewing. Belinda checked her watch for the third time.

"What are you waiting for?" Katie asked as she knotted her thread and reached for another frock to alter.

"Jeff should be calling soon."

"Oh. How are things going with him? Have you told your family about him yet?"

"They know and they're not happy. They don't want him to come back here again to see me. It's so unfair."

"I figured that might have been the problem when he didn't show up last week-end. That's a shame. I know it's got to be hard on you to be separated like this."

"It may not be any better when I go back home. My parents are unbending about us not seeing each other.

Katie, I don't know what we're going to do! We may have to just go off and elope."

"Oh, that would be horrible. Then no one would speak to you. Even his folks would get mad, I bet."

"They're mad enough as it is. They had a long talk with Jeff and made it clear that they were totally against us marrying."

"Wow. That's rough. What's going to happen?"

"I wish I knew. All I know, is that we love each other and we can't be apart. How it all turns out is anyone's guess."

"It's a tough decision. I know how strongly you feel about remaining Amish."

"How strongly I *used* to feel. At this point, I don't care about anything."

"You have to keep your head together, Belinda, and not do anything rash. Your family will always be important to you. Look at my Aunt Esther. She's still ignored by some of the people around here, even after all these years."

"But she's not sorry she left, is she?"

"I don't know for sure. She admits it was a tough decision and quite frankly, I think she's had her moments."

"Of course that was a long time ago and now she's married to a nice man and she has a good profession. So all in all, it worked out all right for her."

"But Belinda, you don't have a strong desire to have a fancy career or see the world, do you?"

"Nee. I've seen enough of this world to be quite content to remain in Ohio someday—or even here. I like Pennsylvania. But if it's the only way I can be together with Jeff, I would consider leaving. He's going to be a Mennonite now, you know. I would think that would be enough for my parents. After all, they're plain people, too."

"It depends on your bishop. Is he real strict?"

"He's fairly new. I don't know him that well. He's such a somber man. His wife is nice, though. She's expecting their eighth boppli this month."

"I think you should go talk to him when you get home. Maybe he wouldn't ban you. You don't know."

"That's a gut idea. I'm gonna do that. Do you want help with your mending? I'm just making pot holders because I'm bored."

"I'm nearly done, but danki."

Belinda sighed and resumed her crocheting. It was not something she enjoyed doing, but 'idle hands…'

Katie looked over. "You know, Mamm is much better now, and Hannah's going to watch Nathanael three afternoons a week so Ruthie can come over and help. Plus my medicine should be working soon and I should feel stronger. I think you could go home before Thanksgiving, if you want to."

"Really?" Belinda looked over and smiled. "I'd be real happy if I could be home in time for the holidays, but I won't leave you as long as you need me."

"I know, and we all really appreciate what you're doing. I'll miss you when you do leave. You're more like a sister all the time."

"That's the nicest thing you've ever said." Belinda leaned over and squeezed Katie's hand. "We will have to stay in touch."

"So there's another reason to avoid the ban!" She smiled and returned to her dress.

"I hear the phone, Katie, so I'll talk to you later."

"Jah. Say hallo for me."

Belinda removed the ringing phone from her apron pocket and nearly ran into the dawdi haus to have her nightly conversation with Jeff. It was the highlight of her day.

After Jeff got off the phone, he went back to the kitchen for a glass of orange juice before turning in. His eyes were blurry from all the studying he'd done earlier. Carrie was dishing out a bowl of chocolate ice cream for herself when he appeared.

He looked over and smiled. "Hey, save some for me."

She grinned back, removed another dish from the cabinet and handed it over to him while she stood by the sink to eat.

After placing three large scoops in his bowl, he replaced the remaining ice cream in the freezer and leaned against the counter. "Carrie, you're never home anymore. I haven't even seen you since your big date with Dan, the man. How did that go?"

"As you predicted. I'm done with him."

"See? A leopard doesn't change his stripes."

"Spots," she corrected, with a wink.

"What was the turning point?"

"Everything he said and did. He took me for a fool, spewing his flattery like I'd end up falling all over him. It was sickening. Sorry it took so long for me to see him as he is."

"At least you do now. I admit I'm relieved."

"You know, from knowing Belinda and some of her friends and family from Pennsylvania, I have a lot more respect for their way of life. If you still want me to, I'd like to go to the Meetinghouse with you tomorrow. There's something to be said for a simpler, purer life."

Jeff grinned over at his sister. "Come on. Sit."

They sat across from each other and he continued to beam at her while she spooned the ice cream into her mouth. "Carrie, I'd love to have you come with me. In fact, I'd like to have you meet Randy. He's a real good friend and happens to be single."

"Jeffy, no way. Don't play matchmaker with me. I can get my own dates."

"I know that, but it wouldn't hurt to be around guys who see you as a person, instead of a thing. Know what I mean?"

"Only too well. I'm perfectly happy to meet anyone and everyone you know, but as far as fixing me up? No, lay off that area. Right now I want to concentrate on my studies. Next semester I'm taking some courses I'll need if I switch to nursing. That way I'll be ahead a little. Men are not in my viewfinder at the moment and I'd like to keep it that way."

"That's a first," Jeff said, giving his lopsided grin.

"So when do you think Belinda will be back? It's got to be rough on you two."

"It is, but she was talking to Katie today and they're thinking about November sometime. Before Thanksgiving."

"Great! Do you think you'll be invited to her place for Thanksgiving?"

"Not a chance. I burned all those bridges by telling her parents the truth about us. I should have kept my mouth shut."

"That would be a first for you, bro."

"Ha. Ha. Carrie, what would you think if I joined the Amish?"

"Whoa! Way too fast. It's one thing to become a Mennonite, but Amish? Are you serious?"

"If that's the only way we can get married, I'd consider it."

"You don't know that much about it."

"True, but I'm going to try to hook up with a friend of Randy's who's Amish. I wouldn't change over unless I really believed in it. But I am open to thinking about it."

"You must really be in love to consider that major a life-style change. I wonder if I'll ever have a guy that in love with me. I envy her in a way."

"Don't envy her. She's going through a lot right now. It would have been easier on each of us if we'd never met."

"That's a weird thing to say, but I think I know what you mean."

"Anyway, we did, so it's strictly a hypothetical. Besides, I've never felt like this before."

She placed her hand on his. "I know. I love to see you so happy. Trouble is, now you have all these problems connected to it."

"I do, but I'm staying connected to God in a major way. He'll work things out."

"In his timing?"

"Who else's? I'm learning patience, but it isn't easy."

"Tell me about it. Right now all I want is to be a nurse. Like immediately. Afraid it doesn't work like that."

"No, but to have that strong a desire—I believe you're in God's will. You'll be a super nurse."

"Thanks, bro. Now I'm heading for bed." She rose and placed her empty bowl in the dishwasher. "Back to school tomorrow after church. Love you, Jeff."

"Yeah, me too."

As he closed his Bible and turned out the light he spoke to God about his situation.

This is complicated, Lord. I have no idea how it's going to end up, so I'm just going to leave it up to you. Your will be done. Within moments, he was asleep.

Chapter Twenty-Six
Lancaster County, Pennsylvania

After leaving the doctor's office, Leroy and Mary took Katie over to an ice cream parlor for a treat. There was something to celebrate. The latest blood tests showed a slight improvement in the cell count. Slight, but it was a sign to them she was on the mend. Katie's smile was a reward to her family. She was filled with hope.

"Daed said he'll wait around while we pick out new fabric for you, Katie. I want to make a dress that fits you real gut. Holidays are coming up and you still look lost in your old ones."

"I'll probably gain a little as I'm able to eat more," Katie said, though the thought of a new dress was appealing. "I'm thinking of green. A dark green."

"Jah, that would be nice. You're sure you don't mind hanging around, Leroy?"

"Nee, I'll walk over to see Jeremiah. He told me they're making improvements to their buggy line. Wouldn't hurt to check it out."

"Oh, we'll end up waitin' on you, if you go over there," Mary said with a grin.

After leaving the ice cream shop, Mary and Katie went into their favorite fabric shop. Mary's cousin waited on them. "So when's the big day, Katie?" she asked. "I heard you've been keeping it a secret."

Katie's faced blanched and she reached for the counter to steady herself. "There ain't a big day coming—for me," she said, stumbling for the words.

"That's funny. I heard only yesterday—"

"Must have been a rumor," Mary said quickly. "You know how that is."

"Jah. Too many tongues flippin' around. I have a deeper green over on the shelf there, Katie. Go take a look. You're gettin' skinny. You sure won't need much fabric."

Katie walked over and slid her hand between the rows of the cotton cloth. "Nice. Okay, I think this will do."

Mary walked over quickly to retrieve the bolt. "Here, I'll carry it, Katie." She brought it over and laid it on the wide counter.

"Not feelin' gut?" the cousin asked.

"A little weak, is all."

The woman clucked and shook her head. "Girls all want to be like flagpoles. Silly, if you ask me. Most men like a little flesh on their women so they look like women, I betcha."

Mary laughed. "My Katie's been under the weather. She'll plump up again."

"Mudder! I don't want to 'plump up' too much. I used to be like a sofa."

The women laughed as Mary's cousin measured out the proper amount and cut it off the bolt.

Once they got outside, they saw Leroy standing next to the buggy, chatting with two friends from church. They tipped their hats when the ladies arrived and then the family headed for home.

Belinda greeted them at the door with a frown. "Oma wouldn't get out of bed while you were gone. She said it hurts too much on her back. I didn't know what to do. I had to change her pads twice."

Mary removed her shawl and headed for her mother's room. Oma had her head turned toward the wall and didn't answer the daughter at first. "Mamm, you have to get up. You know that. The doctor said you're getting too weak."

Oma finally rolled over and faced her daughter. "I can't do it, Mary. Please understand. I'm just too weak and old to keep fighting."

"Nee. You have to try, Mamm. You don't have any choice. In time, you'll get your strength back, but it's going to take more effort on your part."

Tears ran down the old lady's cheeks. Mary wiped them with a tissue. "Oh, Mamm, don't give up. We need you here with us."

"But I'm such a burden. Look how I've wrecked so many things. No wedding. Belinda has to be away from home. You're sickly and worn out. Why don't the gut Lord just take me home? I want to be with your Daed. I know he misses me."

Mary put her head in her hands. *Oh Lord, help me find the right words.* "Mamm, it's not your fault about Josiah and Katie breaking off. It was their decision. And I'm better now. Look at me. I even went shopping today. Belinda may go back to Ohio in a week or two. See? Things are getting much better and so will you. We'll get you up more frequently for short periods of time until you're stronger. Ruthie's boppli will be here soon and Hannah's, too. Won't that be fun?" Her voice was raised now and her words came out too quickly—too forceful. She consciously slowed down and took several deep breaths.

"Look at you, Mary. You're all tensed up like an over-wound clock. I did this to you."

"Mamm. Stop it! I won't listen any more. You can't give up. That's all there is to it. Now I'm going to get you up and you're going to sit with us at supper."

"My, my. You're a spicy little Amish girl, aren't you?" Mary's frown turned to shared laughter as she went to get Belinda's help.

Josiah checked the marked calendar for the umpteenth time. He had given Katie a date, but it wouldn't hurt to hasten it a little. She'd had plenty of time to think about his letter. If she was weakening, it wouldn't harm his chances to talk to her now. It was nearly four. They'd be preparing supper by now. Maybe he'd get an invitation. He was mighty tired of sandwiches. If not, well, so be it, at least he might get a chance to see his Katie, even if she was still mad at him.

After bathing, brushing his teeth, and shaving, he put on fresh clothing and headed for his covered buggy. Maybe he could talk her into going for a drive. Then they could discuss their future—if they had one. He licked his lips as he ran through all the things he planned to tell her. It wouldn't be easy if she was still upset, but he wasn't about to give up on her. His whole future was based upon their marriage taking place. Surely God had his hand on things. He was probably tired of hearing Josiah's appeals by now.

When he got to the Zook farm, he spotted Wayne, who was grooming his horse. Wayne waved and after tethering his horse, Josiah walked over to him. "Hey, Wayne, how's it going?"

"Gut. And you?"

"Okay, I guess. Is Katie inside?"

"Jah, she's helping with supper."

"Mind if I go in?"

"I don't mind, but I don't know about Katie."

"Jah, I know. She's probably still mad at me."

"I think so. Jah, I'm pretty sure she is, but you can try."

Josiah nodded and attempted a weak smile. Then he went over to the back porch, his heart thumping to beat the band. Goodness, that girl had a strong power over him.

After a faint knock, Katie herself opened the door. Her mouth dropped open and she stood absolutely motionless, her hand still on the knob.

"Can I come in, Katie?"

She opened the door wider and stood back, still expressionless. Belinda and Mary stopped setting the table and stared at him.

Then Mary found her voice. "Hallo, Josiah. Nice to see you. Want some kaffi?"

"Nee, I won't be long." He removed his hat and looked over at Katie. "I just wondered if you'd like to go for a buggy ride, Katie. A short one."

"Nee, I don't think so." She began to fold napkins, but her shaking hands gave her away.

"Well, maybe we can take a short walk," he suggested.

"I'm too tired for a walk."

Mary and Belinda exchanged glances and Mary mentioned she needed Belinda's help in Oma's room. They scooted out before Katie had a chance to object.

The two stood facing each other. Finally, Katie sat down and motioned for him to take a seat across from her.

"Did you read my letter?"

She nodded.

"Is that all you can do, Katie? Just nod? I poured my heart out to you. I meant every word. I'll never forgive myself for hurting you, even though I never meant to."

"I know."

"I think you still care about me. Am I right, Katie?"

"I don't know what I feel."

"Give me a chance. Please let me come by and see you again. We don't have to talk serious. We can start out as friends again. Okay? Will you let me come by?"

Katie shook her head slowly. Tears welled up, then spilled over, running down her cheeks onto her apron.

Josiah reached across the table for her hand, but she lowered her arm and clutched her apron. He stood up and came around to her side of the table and knelt beside her. She turned away from him, but stayed seated.

"Katie, Katie, I love you so. Don't turn away from me. Let me hold you. Please."

"I can't, Josiah. I just can't. Please go away. I have to go lie down. I'm ever so tired."

"Oh, honey, why can't you forgive me? I know you still care. I just know it."

"Jah, I do, but I can't see you again. Don't ask me anymore questions. Please, if you really love me, you'll leave and won't come back."

He remained on his knees for several more moments and then rose and headed for the door. "Katie, I can't say I'll never come back. It would be impossible, but I'll leave you today. I'm not giving up, though. Not in a million years."

The door closed behind him and Katie made her way up the stairs to her refuge. If he only knew, he'd never attempt to see her again. She was a barren Amish woman doomed to never marry.

Chapter Twenty-Seven
Holmes County, Ohio

Carrie and Jeff walked out of the Meetinghouse after services Sunday morning and were greeted by Randy and three other young men whom Jeff knew. After introductions, Randy walked next to Carrie as they headed for their car.

"What did you think of the service?"

"Nice. I really enjoyed it. Your pastor gives a good sermon."

"He does. Think you'll come back?"

"Maybe. Now that my brother's involved."

"Jeff's a great guy. We're glad he's joining the church. Incidentally, next Saturday, the singles are having a get-together here. Potluck and then we'll watch a movie about some missionary workers. I'd love to have you come—as my guest, if you want."

"That might be fun. Sure. What time?"

"It starts at six. How about if I pick you up at your house at half past five."

"Sounds like a plan." She smiled at him—almost shyly. His pleasant demeanor was wholesome. Nothing sexual about his eye contact. She felt perfectly safe with him. A far cry from some of the guys she'd dated. He had thick black wavy hair and dark brown eyes. He was slightly shorter than her brother, but had a nice average physique. She could tell he was probably a runner or some kind of athlete by his lack of extra flesh. All in all, he was an attractive young man, though she'd never call him handsome.

After Jeff joined her in the car, they went back to the house. As they reached the garage, their parents pulled up beside them and waved.

Their mother, Linda, opened her window. "Dad wants to take me out for dinner. Do you want to join us before you head out, Carrie? You, too, Jeff. Why don't you both come along?"

They looked at each other and Carrie shrugged. "I have to eat something before I take off anyway. Sure."

Their mother climbed out of the car, followed by her husband. "I think I'll change my shoes first," she said. "But we should leave in the next fifteen minutes. The restaurant gets busy on Sundays and I know you're in a hurry to leave for school, Carrie."

"That's fine. I'm gonna change into casual clothes."

"I thought you were wearing casual," her father remarked, scanning her tight beige denim pants and black pull-over sweater.

"Daaadd. This is dressy."

He laughed and shook his head. "In my day, the girls—"

"Yeah, I know—all wore beautiful dresses with high heels and stockings. I've heard it before."

"Well, they looked real nice. Your mother was the prettiest of all."

Linda smiled over at her husband. "Not really. Your eyesight was off."

He put his arm around her waist and kissed her cheek as they headed into the house to change.

Jeff went upstairs to add a sweater. He thought about his parents' relationship. They were still close after all these years. Of course, they'd grown up as neighbors, attended the same church and schools, and their families got together frequently for picnics and birthday parties. They shared the same world. No conflicts there. It was a foregone conclusion they'd one day marry. Unfortunately, his life was slightly more complicated than his parents. For a brief moment, he wished he'd found a girl in his group. Fewer problems, but it wasn't meant to be. No, the Lord had brought him together with Belinda and God did not make mistakes. It might be a rough road, but she was worth every pothole along the way.

Lancaster County, Pennsylvania

After church service, Becky came back to the Zook's place to spend time with Katie. Wayne stopped her on the way into the house and mentioned taking a buggy ride later with Katie to get her out of the house. It was a crisp fall day, the sky cloudless and a deep azure blue. Perfect for a ride through the hills and valleys of Lancaster County. Katie was excited to go and invited Belinda, who decided against it, since Oma had been emotional all morning and she and Mary had decided to bundle her up and had encouraged her to sit on the porch while the sun was at its warmest.

Katie sat in the front of the buggy with her brother, at the insistence of Becky, who sat behind Wayne. She looked out the side window. The horse quickened his gait as they found an open back road. The clippity-cloppity sounds of his shoed hooves were hypnotizing to Becky. She sat silently enjoying the scenery while Katie and Wayne bantered back and forth about silly things they spotted alongside the road. It was music to her ears to hear her good friends enjoying a light moment. After so much sorrow in Katie's young life, it encouraged Becky to see she was adjusting to her situation. She'd be so much happier if she'd allow Josiah back in her life. Why was she so stubborn?

When they returned an hour later, Katie excused herself for a nap. Wayne asked Becky if she wanted to walk over to the barn with him while he checked one of the ewes. He feared the animal might be ill by the way she was acting. When they arrived he went over and patted the animal gently, speaking softly in her ear. "How you doing, Milly? Eat anything yet?" He looked over at her food trough. "Gut girl. I see you did eat something."

He turned toward Becky and grinned. "She's a gut ole girl. She's produced a dozen lambs for us."

"She's a nice one. You really like animals, don't you?"

"Oh, jah, they never give me any flack."

Becky let out a laugh. "Does anyone?"

"Everyone!"

"Even me?"

He cocked his head to the side. "Mmm. Let me think that one over. I guess, not lately."

"That's gut. I try to stay out of trouble."

"Want to go for a walk down to the creek?"

"Sure. It's so nice out today. I love the fall, but I'm dreading winter."

"Why? It's a beautiful time of year."

"I don't like being cold."

"Well, jah, that could be a problem."

They walked nearly a half-mile to a creek that ran at the end of the next property. When they got to the bank, Wayne found some small smooth rocks and skimmed them along the surface at the widest spot of the stream. Then he spread his jacket on a large boulder and motioned for Becky to sit. She complied and he dropped down on the grass beside her, folding his arms around his bent legs. "It's quiet by the water. I like to come sometimes to think. I've spent a lot of time here lately—thinking about Katie and all."

"She said her tests came back showing some improvement. That must be encouraging."

"Jah, it is." He picked up another small stone and without rising, tossed it into the water. It plunked and formed a slight spray and rivulets. "I'm still worried about her, though. Leukemia is a real bad disease. That's for sure."

Becky nodded, her smile drawn down now. "She's young and strong, Wayne."

"I've seen young and strong people die from stuff like that."

"We can't think like way. You have to have faith and be optimistic."

"You're right, it's just hard sometimes. I'd feel better if Josiah was still in the picture."

"According to Katie, he wants to come back."

"Then why is she so stubborn? It's not like her to be unforgiving."

"She has her reasons."

He turned toward her and his brows rose. "What reasons?"

"Mainly the fact that she might not be able to have boppli."

"I didn't know that. Wow. That ain't gut."

"She doesn't want him to feel obligated to come back, so she just stays clear of the whole situation."

"Becky, tell me the truth. Does she still love him?"

"Jah. She's admitted it to me."

"I think it's foolishness not to tell him then. Maybe not having kinner would make a difference in his feelings. Who knows? He might take off, but he loves her—she loves him. Seems to me they could work something out. Maybe they could adopt."

"I know. I agree with you. I think she's making a huge mistake by keeping her illness a secret."

"*I* could tell him. This way, if he decides he doesn't want to get involved again because of the baby thing, he wouldn't have to tell her. He could just stay away and in time she'd probably get over him. What do you think?"

"That's a big step. You know she's sworn me to secrecy and—"

"She didn't make me swear. She only mentioned it once. I don't feel I'd be betraying her if I went and talked to him."

"Do it, then, Wayne. It may be the only way they'll get back together. And as you say, if he doesn't want to deal with her situation, it will help him get on with his life, as well."

"Danki for being such a gut friend to Katie. She needs her friends and family to support her through this. I appreciate it, Becky."

Becky nodded. "She'll always be like a sister to me."

"Goodness. Does that mean I'm like a brother?" His grin spread across his face.

"I hope not."

"Jah, me, too. Let's get back. I have to help my daed with the milking soon."

He reached over and took her hand, helping her to a standing position. For a brief second, she wished he'd take her in his arms, but instead he dropped her hand and pointed to the path. She walked ahead of him on the narrow open area and when they came to the road he walked beside her—on the outside to protect her. She liked that. In fact, she liked everything about him. Her feelings had not waned from the time she was a child visiting her friend. Another young man had shown real interest in her, but she had no desire to date anyone else.

Wayne had matured a lot over the last couple years, but so had she. Perhaps in time, he would see her for the woman she had become, not just an annoying kid who came to play with his sister.

Chapter Twenty-Eight
Holmes County, Ohio

Jeff met with Randy for coffee and donuts on Saturday morning. His workload had lessoned and he had called Randy, hoping to get together with his Amish friend. They sat and talked about the differences between the Mennonite and Amish beliefs.

"Some of the Amish don't believe their place in Heaven is secure just by professing belief in Christ. They lean heavily on works. Of course, we Mennonites are strong believers in missionary work, as you know." Randy broke a small piece of his sugar donut and dipped in the hot coffee.

"Yeah, I've talked to Belinda. She feels confident that she's saved through Christ's blood on the cross and her firm conviction that He is the Son of God. She didn't know the term, 'born again,' but basically, that's what she is. She's such a wonderful Christian woman. I really feel blessed to have her in my life."

Randy grinned over at him. "I have to meet her someday. When is she coming back?"

"She hopes to be home for Thanksgiving or right after."

"If she's back in time, will you have dinner with her family?"

"There's no way. We aren't supposed to see each other again. Her family is adamant. I don't know how we're going to manage things when she gets home. I just know I can't stop seeing her altogether. It's gonna be tough."

"I don't envy you. That would be rough. So you're really considering the Amish way of life now? What's the matter, are we too easy on you?"

Jeff laughed. "I was hoping it would be acceptable for us both to be Mennonite and still allow Belinda to be part of her Amish community."

"It doesn't work that way, I'm afraid. Maybe in some areas. Things are changing throughout the country, but around here, they're still pretty strict. Has Belinda taking her kneeling vows yet?"

"No. She was going to, but thankfully, she hadn't gotten that far."

"That's a plus. At least I don't believe she'd be shunned. Not officially, anyway, but there will be people who won't understand and will probably ignore her once you two marry. That is, if you don't become Amish yourself." Randy popped the rest of his donut in his mouth and checked his watch. "Now would be a good time to stop by and see Levi. The milking should be completed by now. Done?"

"Yep. All set. We can go in one car if you want."

"No, we should take both cars, because you'll want to stay longer and talk, if he's able to give you the time."

Jeff followed his friend as he wound through the countryside. Eventually, he put his turn signal on and headed down a long lane to a farmhouse. Levi lived in a remote part of the county on two hundred acres of gently rolling hills. It was a picture of paradise and Jeff's heart swelled when he realized he could live that way himself someday. Maybe.

When they pulled in, Jeff noted about five or six young boys playing softball in the back yard. There were two young toddlers building Legos on the back porch. After being introduced to Levi's wife, they headed into the barn where they found Levi sitting on a bale of hay talking to another Amish man about the same age as he was. Levi greeted Randy with a wide smile and a smack to his arm. Then they were introduced to his friend, Mo, who was puffing on a corncob pipe. It was mild for November, but Jeff was glad he'd worn a sweater since it was cool in the barn.

After Mo and Randy left, Levi took Jeff back to his kitchen where he served him a large mug of hot cider. His wife, Alice, tended to her new baby and left the men to discuss things alone.

"So Randy tells me you're a new Mennonite."

"Yes, I've gone through instruction and I'm now going to join the church."

He nodded and reached for a gingersnap, after offering one to Jeff.

"And why do you want to learn about our ways? Ain't tough enough on you to be Mennonite?" He grinned and his ginger beard grazed his wool jacket.

"It's not that. I guess I should explain. I'm engaged to an Amish girl, but her parents aren't too happy about it."

"I bet you got that right. We have a pretty closed society, you know."

"I know, but there's a lot I like about your way of life."

"It's mighty hard work."

"I'm not afraid of work. In fact, I want to farm eventually. Right now I'm working for a landscaper. It's possible I could have my own business some day. But all that is incidental."

"What do you want from me?"

"I was hoping I could stop by sometimes and you could explain about the Ordnung. My girlfriend has told me a lot, but she's gotten most of her information from her parents and actually hasn't read the whole rule book herself yet."

"Many of us haven't," he said with a crooked grin. "But we're trained from pups to do things the old way. It's kinda second nature. I ain't even comfortable in the city or amongst just the Englishers. No offence."

Jeff smiled. "None taken. I'm not nuts about cities myself. Give me the country any day."

"When do you want to start?"

"Anytime."

"Now?"

"If you have time."

"You have to follow me around. I have to feed the chickens. I like to give my kinner off part of Saturday. They're gut kids and work hard, but they sure like playtime, that's for sure."

The rest of Jeff's morning was spent trailing behind Levi, filling out a pad with a multitude of notes. Much of the information would be easy to follow.

"So I guess that should do it for now," Levi announced, returning a shovel to the barn. "How bout next Saturday. Same thing?"

"That would be great. I'd like to pay you for—"

"For what I like to do best? Gab? Nee, I'm happy to do it. You wouldn't wanna tell me the lucky girl's name, would you? I might know the family."

"Please don't take it wrong, but I'd like to do all this in private for now. You'll be first on the wedding invitation list, though, if it happens. I should say, *when* it happens."

Levi extended his hand. "I hope it works out for you. From what I can see, you might not have a hard time being Amish. I can tell you're an honest man by your eyes."

"Thanks, or should I say 'danki'?"

Levi laughed and they shook hands. "Same time next week."

Jeff walked back to his car with his notepad bulging with information. Funny, now he wondered if he'd be the one to get shunned.

Lancaster County, Pennsylvania

Mary and Belinda helped Oma out of the tub in the kitchen. Heat poured out of the coal stove warming the room, though she still stood shivering as they wrapped her in large towels and guided her back into her makeshift bedroom on the same level.

"I don't know why I have so many baths. It ain't like I'm out running around," she stated.

"Mamm, it's important to bathe, especially with your problems."

"Wearing diapers, you mean? You take real gut care of me, you girls. I don't know what I'd do without you." She sat on the bed and Belinda sprinkled her back with baby powder and smoothed it over her bony frame.

"We can't let you get bed-sores," she said handing the container over to Mary, who powdered her mother's front and legs.

"There, now don't you smell pretty."

"I like my lavender water, too, Mary."

"Jah, I can't forget that." She patted her mother's wrists with the homemade lavender water and lifted her legs onto the mattress while Belinda arranged the bed pillows under her head.

"Now, I think I'll sleep a little while, if it's okay."

"Jah, I imagine we gave you quite a work-out," Mary said with a grin. After pulling down the shades, they returned to the kitchen.

"Want to run the stairs up and see if Katie wants tea?" Mary asked Belinda.

"Sure. Let me check." Belinda made her way up to Katie's room and heard her singing softly. She knocked on the door. When she entered, Katie was sitting on her bed and had her Bible in her lap. She seemed embarrassed to be caught singing.

Belinda smiled over. "Sounds gut. You have a nice voice. We're gonna have tea now. Do you want some?"

"Jah, I'll come down. I was just reading Psalm 28. I love the part where it says...wait, I'll read it. 'The Lord is my strength and my shield; my heart trusts in him and I am helped. My heart leaps for joy and I will give thanks to him in song.' That's what I was doing, Belinda. God has drawn me so close to Himself through all this stuff I'm going through. He really has been my strength. Do you know what I mean?"

Belinda sat on the bed next to her and folded her arms. "I think so. I've had to lean on Him more now, too, what with all the problems I'm having with my situation with Jeff. It's like—who do you turn to, if you don't have God?"

"That's what I mean. Do you get comfort?"

"Jah. I pray a lot more now and feel closer to Him. I still miss Jeff tons, but I think things are going to be okay someday. Not only for me, but for you, Katie. God will take care of you."

Katie nodded and set her Bible on the table next to her bed. "The doctor didn't say I definitely couldn't have boppli—just that sometimes it's harder. Maybe I've been too pessimistic."

"Maybe so. It's not the end of the world if you *can't* have boppli. Think about all the unloved children in the world. Maybe you could adopt kinner if you can't have your own."

"Jah, I'd do that. But I wouldn't want to do it alone."

"Of course not. You'll get married someday."

"Just not to Josiah." She put her head back on her pillow and twisted her kapp ribbon. "Enough about me. Let's go down and have our tea. I'm gonna miss you when you leave."

"I may go this week-end, if everything is okay here."

"Is Jeff picking you up?"

Belinda let out a long sigh. "Nee. Daed talked to Onkel Leroy last night and he's getting our regular driver. I'm so disappointed."

"That's a shame. I hope your parents come around. After all, if Jeff's gonna be a Mennonite, they're plain like us."

"Not plain enough, I fear."

"Nee," Katie said with a grin. "We're definitely the plainest of all, if that's not being too conceited." They went down to join Mary for tea and fresh bread pudding.

Chapter Twenty-Nine
Lancaster County, Pennsylvania

Mary hung up and handed the cell phone over to Belinda, as they sat in the living room. "I can't stand using that thing. I have trouble understanding people's words. I think they talk too fast. Esther insists on phoning."

Belinda smiled and set the phone back on the mantle. "But it's a nice way to stay in touch. Is your schwester coming for Thanksgiving?"

"Jah, Esther and her husband will come in Wednesday. She wants to make the chestnut stuffing for the turkeys. It's the only thing she remembers doing from her days living home."

Belinda smiled. "I don't even know how to do that yet. Mamm always prepares it. My sister, Rachel, cooks real gut, but I have a lot to learn."

"I like your cookies," Mary said.

"How are you going to manage when I go back to Ohio? You know, I can stay on awhile longer if you need me."

"Danki, I appreciate your offer, but I'm feeling gut now and Katie's getting over some of her reaction to the medication. She can help a little. Ruthie and Emma are going to take turns with the wash and Wayne even offered to help, so you see, we'll be just fine."

"I hope Oma gets stronger."

"I think she's trying a little harder, poor dear. I know her will to live ain't what it should be, but who can blame her?"

Belinda nodded. "Jah, it's real sad."

She heard the kitchen door open and Wayne called out. "Where is everybody?"

"In the living room, sohn. Come in here."

He walked in and nodded toward Belinda. "I just wanted to tell you I'm going off for a while. Daed went next door to see Abram. He came by and said he needed help with something."

"Don't you need to help also?"

"Nee, Abram said it was advice, not brawn," he said, grinning over at Belinda.

"Let me know when you're back and I'll start kaffi," Mary suggested. He nodded and left.

"Guess I'll start the laundry," Belinda said, rising from her chair. "Only two sets of sheets today."

Mary shook her head. "You're a wonderful-gut helper, Belinda. Your parents should be pleased with you."

"Not pleased enough to let me choose the man I want to marry."

"If he were Amish…"

"I'm afraid that ain't gonna happen."

"Belinda, what if they don't accept him? Would you break it off?"

"I can't. I'm too far gone. I'll never love another man the way I love him. I'll leave the Amish if that's the only way around it."

"Oh, mercy. That would be so sad."

"Esther seems happy."

"She ain't always been that happy. She told me herself she had some hard days."

"You can have hard days even if you stay Amish."

Mary's lips turned up. "Oh, jah, you can say that again. Well I'm praying things will work out for you, Belinda."

"Danki. I trust God is in control and it will be in His timing."

"Gut way to think about it. Jah, His timing ain't always in agreement with ours. Let me go start the chicken for dinner."

Wayne noticed Josiah was chopping firewood by the barn when he pulled in. Josiah looked up in surprise when he noted Wayne jump down from the buggy. After securing his horse, he and Josiah headed for the house.

"Nothing wrong, is there?" Josiah asked as they reached the kitchen door and walked in.

"Just thought I'd come by and have a chat. Haven't seen much of you lately."

"Not the way I'd like it, you know," Josiah said as he took a can of coffee off the shelf and set it on the counter. "Kaffi?"

"Jah. Danki."

"Sit. Let me start a pot and then I'll relax with you." He took his time adding the water to the percolator and measured several scoops into the strainer. He placed it over the gas burner and then sat across from his friend. "So what's going on?"

"I'm taking my chances in coming over to talk to you about Katie. She has no idea I'm here and wouldn't be pleased if she knew."

Josiah sat back and crossed his legs. "What can you say? She's stubborn as a mule about forgiving me. I didn't even do anything that bad."

"There's another reason she's staying away from you."

"Is it another guy?" Josiah's brows creased and his jaw clenched. He wasn't sure he wanted to hear the answer to that question, but he stared over at Wayne waiting for his answer.

"Nee, no one else. She still cares about you and—"

"She has a funny way of showing it."

"Hear me out. Katie is sick. Real sick."

Josiah leaned forward as he gripped the side of the table. "What do you mean? What's wrong with her?"

"She has leukemia."

It was as if he'd been struck with a sledge hammer. He could barely breathe. "Leukemia? That's deadly, ain't it?"

"Apparently her type can be controlled with medication."

"Poor sweet Katie. How long has she known?"

"I'm not sure how long it's been now. It seems like forever that we've been dealing with it."

"Why does she keep me away? I want to be with her and help her through this. Wayne, will she get better?" His eyes connected with Wayne's as he searched for more information.

"Her doctor says he thinks it can be controlled with medication. They want to get it into remission. The medicine made her real sick in the beginning but she told me she's feeling better lately."

"I still don't understand why she didn't tell me. I have to go over right now."

"Wait, there's more."

Josiah leaned forward and waited.

"She may not be able to have boppli."

Josiah sat back in his chair and stared at Wayne.

Wayne continued. "That's one reason she doesn't want you back. She believes you deserve a wife who can give you the kinner you deserve."

"Those were her words?"

"Pretty much. Belinda's close to her now and so is Becky, of course. They've tried to talk her into getting together with you again, but she insists it wouldn't be fair to you. She words it—'to an incomplete woman.'"

Josiah placed his head in his hands and shook his head. "Of course I want my own children. Every man does, but Katie comes first. I can't imagine being married to anyone else. I have to convince her it wouldn't matter."

"You'd better pray about it first. Maybe it matters more than you realize. It could be a major issue. I felt if I told you first—before she did, which would be inevitable—then you could make the right decision for your own future. No one could blame you if you just drew away. She wouldn't even have to know why, since you two are on the outs anyway."

"I know right now. I want to marry Katie no matter what's wrong."

Wayne reached across the table and patted his arm. "Look, just don't rush right over. Please take your time and pray about this whole thing. I know right now you think you can't live without Katie, but you can't make the wrong decision. To come back and then decide later on that being a father is a factor, well, it could hurt her more in the end."

Josiah nodded. "I guess that makes sense. I'll pray about it, and ponder everything before I do anything more. Right now, I just want to go and hold her and protect her, but you're right. I need to be absolutely sure I can go through with everything. If I didn't love kids so much, I wouldn't even have to think about it. But I've always pictured my life with a dozen little ones running around. Of course, we could adopt."

"Jah, true. Even foster care."

Josiah stood and turned the flame down under the percolator. "I hope you can stay for kaffi, Wayne. Look, I really appreciate you coming here like this. I'm surprised no one seems to know about Katie. Our friends and all— no one's said a word."

"She wanted to keep it that way. Mainly so you wouldn't find out."

"She's doing that for me, ain't she? She still puts everyone else above herself. That's my Katie."

Wayne nodded. "She's a gut person. I feel awful bad for her right now, but she's showing real strength."

"That's gotta come from God. With all she's been through lately…"

"That's for certain. Jah, I could use a cup of brew. It's been quite a morning."

As Wayne headed home, he prayed he'd done the right thing. The ball was in Josiah's court now. God only knows, Wayne prayed he would make the right decision—for all concerned.

Holmes County, Ohio

"I have a driver set up for Tuesday, Grace. Belinda can be home for Thanksgiving. What do you think?"

"What do I think? I think it's wonderful! I can't wait to have her home again. We'll have a houseful."

"I hope she ain't gonna complain about not seeing Jeff."

"She'll get over it. I'll invite Rebecca Smucker and her whole family. Zeke has a case on her and maybe we can get things moving."

"Honey, she's got her heart set on Jeff. Zeke don't stand a chance."

"We'll see. What time will she be here? Any idea?"

"Nee. Probably late afternoon. Dickens likes to leave before dawn. Less traffic that way, but it's still a long trip."

"Well, I hope we don't have any more trouble with that girl. She's head-strong, she is."

"Like her mamm?" Jed put his arms around his wife and kissed her on the cheek. "Seems to me, you got your way a lot when you were her age."

"I got the man I wanted, that's for sure," she replied, kissing him back on his lips.

"I'm sure glad it was me."

After Jed went outside, Grace went up to check Belinda's room. It looked perfect, but just to make sure, she took a dust rag and ran over the furniture to remove any missed particles of dust. She patted Belinda's pillow and visualized her daughter's smile. It had been way too long. There was no way she would survive if her daughter yanked over to the English. No way at all.

Chapter Thirty
Holmes County, Ohio

Jeff couldn't concentrate on his studies. Every time he thought about Belinda's return the next day, he made a different plan. He'd stop by. No, he'd call. They'd meet somewhere. That would be sneaking around—not a good idea. But he had to see her. If he went to her home, he'd have to deal with the wrath of her parents. If they met somewhere else, it would be deception. What kind of Christian would do that? Was she still his fiancé?

When it came right down to it, he was faced with a dilemma. All alternatives were equally frustrating. But see her he must. When he spoke with her the night before, he detected the same sort of confusion in her voice. She, too, was going through identical frustration. The only thing they both agreed upon, they had to see each other. Somewhere. Somehow.

Before heading for bed, Jeff went into the kitchen to grab a half sandwich. His father was sitting at the table reading the newspaper. He looked at his son as he walked in and made his way to the refrigerator.

"Hungry again?"

"Always," he said, smiling over as he removed some sliced ham and cheese from the refrigerator. "Want me to make you a sandwich?"

"No thanks. I just couldn't sleep. I figured a glass of milk might help." He pointed to an empty glass next to

221

his placemat. "I'm afraid part of my reason for insomnia involves you, Jeff."

After adding mustard to his meat and cheese, Jeff placed his snack on a paper napkin and sat across from his father. "What about me?"

"I think you know. You're determination to screw up your life."

"By marrying the girl I love? Or by finding meaning in my spiritual life?"

"Both. You're not using your head. There are plenty of girls you can choose from who are used to the same kind of life you are. And since when is it necessary to drive a black car and wear dull clothes to prove a point?"

"It's their custom. They don't want to be like the rest of America and live to show off how much money they make and dress immodestly. Is there anything wrong with that?" Jeff could feel anger arise, but he tried his utmost to be respectful.

"I think it's a shame the Amish don't let their kids get a decent education. For Pete's sake, why would you want to stay ignorant?"

"They may be uneducated, but they're far from ignorant. I'd like to see most of us live off the land the way they do and be independent of the government. They depend on God and each other and I admire what they're able to maintain with their customs. Divorce is unheard of."

"Is that good? Would you want to be stuck in a bad marriage? What about abuse? Are you trying to tell me they're all saints and there's no such thing as wife or child abuse?"

"I'm sure there are isolated cases, after all they're still human, but on the whole they live good, clean lives. Family means everything to them."

"Apparently, it means more than it does to you. Do you realize how upset your mother is? She's embarrassed to talk with her friends when they ask about you. Janice Townsend called her yesterday and asked if it was you she saw driving that sad-looking car you bought. Looks like a hearse."

"Come on, Dad. You can do better than that. What do I care what that gossip thinks of the car I drive."

"Apparently you don't care about what anyone thinks—including your family."

"Carrie's okay with it. In fact, she likes the Mennonite faith. She went to a young adult event with my friend."

"Leave her out of this. You have too much influence on Carrie. Always have."

"I think I've had a good affect on her. She finally woke up about Dan, thanks to my warning."

"Your mother thinks she made a mistake. The young man has a great future. His family is loaded."

"Like that's real important."

"We're not going to see eye-to-eye on this, it's apparent, but I'd like you to agree not to see that Belinda girl—at least until your schooling is finished."

"Four years? You've got to be kidding."

"Until next summer, anyway. Maybe by then, things will be cooled off and you'll be using your head instead of your heart."

"I can't promise that. She's coming home tomorrow. I have to see her. Have you forgotten what it's like to be in love?"

"Ridiculous! I love your mother more than you'll ever know. But we were perfect for each other. Her world was my world. Sure, we had tiffs and had to work out some minor differences, but we understood each other and were on the same page."

"I don't want friction, Dad. I just want you to give Belinda a chance. I know you'd love her if you'd open yourself up to accept her, because no matter what you think or her parents want, we're going to get married someday."

His father sighed and then stood up. "I guess there's nothing more to say. Just know that I'm not about to invest in a business venture with you if you insist on pursuing this hopeless relationship."

"I realize that. I'm sorry to be a disappointment to you both. Hopefully, someday you'll accept me for who I am and my wife and family as well."

Jeff threw out half the sandwich and made his way up to bed. He no longer felt the need to eat. He decided to read since he knew sleep would evade him.

Nellie spent the morning baking Belinda's favorite potato cake, handed down several generations. She chopped up the nuts as she put the finishing touches in the batter. It amazed her that mashed potatoes could be so good in cake. Grace smiled over as she cut up stew meat for the main meal. Since she didn't expect her daughter's return until late afternoon, the family would eat their main meal at noon, as was their custom, but she'd have enough leftover stew if Belinda was hungry when she arrived home. She put extra carrots in the pot—Belinda's favorite vegetable.

Jed came in from the barn and washed up. "I need a break. Any kaffi left from breakfast?" he asked Grace.

"I'll put a fresh pot on. Just let me finish flouring the meat. Are you excited, Jed?"

"More nervous than excited."

"Why, Daed?" Nellie asked as she poured the batter into greased cake pans.

"You know your schwester. She can be a problem."

"I think she's learned her lesson, Daed. She said she doesn't party anymore. Not since she met... I mean she doesn't care, is all."

"I'm glad about that, but now she's got this case on Jeff. It ain't gonna work for those two. She should give it up."

Nellie nodded. "I told her the same thing, but she really loves him. He's a nice guy."

Grace looked over. "Just not Amish. That's a big problem."

"But if he's gonna be Mennonite, what's the big deal?" Nellie continued questioning as she slid the pans into the hot oven.

"It's a big deal all right, young lady," her mother said. "Learn from her mistakes. Don't get involved with the outside world or you might be tempted as she is. Now Rachel, she never gave us a moment's grief."

"Is she coming over soon?"

"Jah, in about an hour. Reuben's finishing some work first."

"What if Jeff comes by on Thanksgiving? You can't turn him away, can you?"

Jed scowled. "He knows better than to show up uninvited."

"But Belinda could invite him."

"We're going to get a few things straight from the beginning. As far as I'm concerned, Belinda is living under our roof and even though she's nearly eighteen, she lives by our rules."

"Wow! I bet she'll wanna go back to Pennsylvania."

Grace shook her head. "I sure hope not. We need to be a family again."

A few minutes later, Rachel and Reuben came in the back door. Rachel had a large bowl of mixed salad greens and two loaves of fresh rye bread, still warm from the oven. Nellie grabbed the bread and proceeded to cut some up. She placed them in a basket on the table, alongside fresh-whipped butter. The kitchen's odors blended into a mouth-watering bouquet and soon the whole family was seated around the table spreading the bread with the butter, some adding orange marmalade, and enjoying the fruits of Rachel's labor.

"We have some gut news," Rachel remarked as she sipped some homemade cider.

"You're having a boppli?" Nellie asked immediately.

"Hush, Nellie, let your sister talk."

Rachel giggled. "She's right, Mamm. I'm expecting again."

"Well, I'll be. I'm so happy for you both," Grace said, grinning from ear-to-ear.

Reuben blushed as he put his arm around his wife. "She looks real gut and the boppli is due in springtime. May, right honey?"

"Jah, in the warm weather. I'm so excited."

"We have to be cautious, though. We don't want to spread the word just yet. Let's give it another couple months. By then it won't be a secret anyway," he added, as he smiled over at his wife.

"Wait till Belinda hears," Nellie said. "Her first niece. Oh mine, too."

"And my first grandchild. I hope you'll let us spoil it."

"Of course! That's what a grossmammi is for," Rachel said.

Everything was ready now. Nellie stayed close to the window, waiting for Belinda, yet again.

Chapter Thirty-One
Lancaster County, Pennsylvania

Family and friends stopped by all day to say good-bye to Belinda who had packed and prepared for her departure the following day. Word got around quickly and lists were made and calendars marked as to who would stop by to lend Mary and Kate a hand with the many chores once they were on their own.

Oma was unusually quiet all morning, barely speaking to her family who attempted to engage her in conversation. Ruth sat next to her wheelchair, which they'd brought into the living room, and mentioned she was due the following month.

"Jah, you look pretty big, Ruthie," she finally commented. "Bet you don't sleep too gut."

"Nee, but I get up with Nathanael most nights, anyway. He still nurses sometimes, more for comfort than hunger."

"Better put an end to that, or you'll never get any rest. Besides, you need to freshen up before the new one arrives."

"You're right. Actually he hasn't gotten me up for the last three nights. I'm pretty dried up now."

"You hoping for a little *fraulein* this time?"

"It would be ever so nice, but whatever the Lord brings, we'll be happy."

"Your hubby looks well-fed. You take gut care of him."

"I try. He's such a sweetheart. He does most of the vegetable garden himself, along with the fields. All that and his job at the buggy shop, too."

"He's spoiling you."

Ruth nodded. "Jah, he sure does. I guess you're going to miss Belinda. She's been such a help to all of us."

"Jah, she's a honey of a girl. I hope it's not too much for Mary and Katie to take care of me. I'm really trying to get back my strength, but I ain't back to my old self."

"Maybe you expect too much, Oma. You've been through a lot."

"Jah. Too much, if you ask me. I'm ready to join my love."

"Oh, please don't talk like that. You have so many who love you. We want you to stay as long as possible."

"But I'm so much work. I wear diapers now, you know."

"That's no problem. We're Amish. We do for our loved ones and we don't complain."

Belinda walked into the room and sat on the other side of Oma, taking her hand in hers. "I'm going to miss you so much, but I'll come back and visit."

"I hope so, deary. You're my little angel."

Tears formed in Belinda's eyes and she leaned over and kissed the old woman on her cheek.

Emma arrived with the four children and it got crowded in the living room. Oma asked to be put back in her bed, but Lizzy insisted on reading a poem first, which she'd written for Oma. She was given permission to read it out loud.

"White is the color of snowflakes as they fall.
White is the color of Oma's old shawl.

White is the color of dreams when we nap.
And white is the color of my Mammi's kapp,
But pink is the color of my brand new rug,
and pink is the color of Oma's cheeks when we hug."

"Well, you are quite a poet, young lady," Oma said with a grin. So come and make my cheeks pink, *lieb*."

The family smiled as the child folded the poem and placed it in Oma's apron pocket before receiving a hug. "Don't ever lose it, Oma."

"Nee. You couldn't have written it at a better time, Lizzy."

"I know. God gave it to my brain this morning before I even ate breakfast."

"Well, how about that! Danki. I'll treasure it always."

Lizzy's grin stayed pasted on her sweet face all day, though when she and her family left, she became teary when Belinda hugged her goodbye.

Belinda held each of the twins and kissed their soft cheeks before handing them back to Gabe and Emma. She noticed Katie in the background. It was obvious that this was in many ways a difficult day for her. So many little ones—so much joy. What would the future hold for her friend?

After everyone left, Belinda retired to her room early. She had to speak to Jeff. She was excited to be going back to Ohio, but she also feared the future. With so many objections to their relationship, she needed to be reassured by the man she loved.

Jeff picked up on the first ring. "I knew it was you even before I checked the phone. I almost called you first, but I try to wait so you can talk in private. How did your day go?"

"Nice. I'm exhausted, though. We were busy all day, people coming and going. I've made so many new friends here. Even though I've missed you and everyone home, it's been a gut experience. Oh, Jeff, I can't wait to see you."

"Me too. Do you think it would be wrong for me to show up tomorrow night at your house? Maybe I could find a book or something to bring your dad."

"Not tomorrow. I don't want to start off on the wrong foot. My parents are pretty adamant about my not seeing you. But Thanksgiving, maybe you could stop by just to say hallo. Surely, they can't object to that. Maybe you can bring Carrie. It will look like you're just being friendly."

Jeff laughed. "I think your parents won't be fooled by that, honey. I will stop by though. I have to. We've got to work something out so we can be together. Even if it's in a family setting."

"Oh, Jeff, it's so discouraging. Maybe we should just elope and let the chips fall where they may."

"I'd love to marry you right away, but we have to be sensible. It costs money to live and right now I barely make enough to put fuel in the tank and pay the car insurance. I have to buy meals at school and the books cost a lot and—"

"I know. You've explained it before and I know you're right. It's just so hard. I think about you all the time."

"Someday it will all work out. I'm sure of it. We just have to remain fast to our beliefs and things will get better."

"I trust you're right. The driver will be here before noon, so I should get home late afternoon. I'm going to have to hide the phone from the family. I'm determined to keep it so I can at least talk to you everyday."

"How will you re-charge it?"

"I haven't figured that out yet. Here, I just plug it into a generator thingy, but at home I can't let the folks know I have it."

"We'll have to keep our conversations on the short side then. You can go to town every other day maybe and go to a coffee house or something to re-charge it."

"I even feel guilty about that. I feel guilty about everything! I'm sick of feeling this way. All I want is to marry you and have a family. What's so terrible about that?"

"Absolutely nothing."

"I'd better sign off and get some sleep, Jeff. I'll call you tomorrow when I get home then, even if it's just a quick 'hi' and then I hang up. But we'll plan on you coming on Thanksgiving. I just won't mention it to anyone."

"Have a safe trip, honey. I'll be praying for you. See you in two days."

"Gut nacht."

She held the phone against her chest as if somehow she was still connected to him. Then she undressed and prepared for a long night. Tomorrow it would be time to move on.

Holmes County, Ohio

Jeff laid the phone on his desk. He wondered what his reception would be on Thursday when he showed up at her home. Probably not too great, he surmised. But the

Amish would never be downright rude and confront his being there. He'd talk Carrie into going along, since that would make it a bit easier. After all, she and Belinda were close friends. Of course, she'd want to see her after all this time.

It was nice to have a few days off from school. He'd hoped to pick up hours at his landscaping job, but his boss had closed up shop to take a cruise somewhere. Maybe it was just as well. It gave him time to investigate further in his study of Amish living. Levi gave him some articles to read the last time he saw him. So far, there wasn't anything too outrageous. He figured he could adhere to just about any of the rules. The toughest would be getting rid of his computer. Maybe they'd make an exception since he could use it in his business—if he ever had his own, that is. On second thought, they could probably care less about saving him work. People who labor as hard as they do wouldn't be concerned if it took an extra two hours a day to get your desk work in order.

Levi encouraged him to spend more time in Amish homes and get to know the people better. Little did he know that was exactly what he'd like to do? It would be his greatest wish to practically live at the Glick's. What a shame they didn't feel the same way. He smiled when he pictured Belinda's expression if he actually decided to become Amish. He wasn't even sure if they'd accept him. They certainly wouldn't encourage him if they thought his conversion was merely the result of loving an Amish woman. No, that was not reason enough to change over to a completely different life-style. His heart was slowly leaning towards a simpler existence. He believed the Mennonite way of life was the right one for him at this point in time, but if Belinda would be shunned by joining the Mennonite community, he could not ask her to leave.

Her family was too important to her. He would not want the responsibility of causing such a permanent rift in her relationships. There had to be a better way. What it was, he had no idea. Prayer was in order. He found himself in communion frequently with God. If nothing else positive came from this period of his life, at least it had drawn him closer to his maker.

Chapter Thirty-Two
Holmes County, Ohio

It seemed to take forever to get back home. They traveled through several rainstorms, which slowed them down considerably. The driver, Tom Dickens, was a pleasant sort of man, but he became silent when the weather demanded his concentration. It was just as well. It allowed Belinda time to make the transition mentally.

She'd miss everyone back in Pennsylvania, but she was relieved to put an end to her stint and return to her loved ones—especially Jeff. How she missed him. She hungered to hear his laughter again, to feel his strong grip on her hand, and to feel his gentle lips on hers. They'd have to be wary not to spend time alone. There was too much enticement to be close. She now understood the idea of chaperones, common in the past. Young people's hormones were lively and it was all too easy to succumb to temptation if the circumstances allowed it. So the best idea was to control the circumstances. She and Jeff had discussed it once and he was in full agreement. What a wonderful man he was. How fortunate that God had allowed them to meet. What had started as friendship had quickly turned to love. She could never settle for a relationship built merely on affection. The marriage commitment required a deeper emotion.

She was not naive enough to believe it would always be 'cloud nine' since she was a realist as well as a romantic. Watching her parents as they worked through trials, illnesses, and differences, she saw firsthand how a couple must deal with each crisis as it arrived. Fortunately, she also saw how God was involved in every decision and event in her parents' lives. He was the rock they built their home upon, their resting place and their hope. She knew Jeff felt as she did about God and His place in their lives. They were equally yoked, though they came from such different backgrounds. The Lord was the equalizer. Whatever differences they had, they shared the commonality of knowing Christ as their savior. No matter what struggles lay ahead, and there would be many, He would guide them in their decisions and their trials. She bowed her head to give thanks.

Around four, they pulled up to her home. Apparently, it had stormed there also, since puddles were visible and the remaining leaves dangling on the branches glistened from their recent shower. Nellie was the first to welcome her, coming out barefoot from the front door. They embraced and Nellie began to tell her all about their plans for the holiday and mentioned the inclusion of Becky and her family.

That was not the greatest of news. Zeke would be ogling her as usual and if Jeff did show up, there might be the male thing again, causing everyone to be uncomfortable. There was little she could do about it, so she just smiled and walked arm and arm with her little sister toward the house. When they got to the door, Grace and Jed came out to greet her and then Gideon appeared from the barn area and grinned broadly at her, even allowing a sisterly hug. Jed went to retrieve her suitcase and pay the driver and then they all went in together and sat around the table discussing the events and family situations in Pennsylvania.

Nellie was amused at Lizzy's poem, which Belinda had copied for them to read, and Mary had sent a recipe for Grace for a Dutch tomato pudding, which she'd requested after having eaten it during their visit.

Belinda glanced at her watch. Hopefully, she still had enough energy to call Jeff, but she needed to wait until bedtime to make her call.

Finally, it was time to retire for the night. In order not to be heard, she covered herself up with her quilt and spoke in hushed tones. Jeff could barely make out her words, but he sounded excited to hear she'd made it safely. When asked about the time he should make his appearance, she suggested around four, since dinner would be over and even clean-up. They'd have more of an opportunity to talk if he arrived late. Carrie decided to come along, which would help the situation.

"We'll have to make our plans for the rest of the week-end," Jeff added. "Do you think you'd like to meet me at the family restaurant in Bird-in-Hand one afternoon?"

"That sounds like a gut idea. We'll set a time tomorrow. I'm down to thirty percent on my battery. I hope it lasts until we get to town and I find a place to re-charge it."

"Honey, are you okay with all this? You won't feel too guilty going behind your parents' back?"

"I don't have much of a choice. I've been dealing with guilt for a while now. I hate it and I don't want to live this way. If only they'd accept the fact that I'm not going to change my mind about you. It's frustrating."

"How I know. Believe it or not, I'm having the same struggle at this end. It feels like Romeo and Juliet."

"Mercy, that had a bad ending, didn't it?"

"Rather," he said, chuckling. "I won't go there."

After a couple more minutes, they hung up and Belinda settled into her cozy soft mattress. The faint odor of soap mixed with the fresh scent of the outdoors on her pillowcase were all too familiar. It was good to be home. And wonderful to know within twenty-four hours, she'd see Jeff.

Lancaster County, Pennsylvania

Josiah combed his hair back, adding a little water to tame his unruly waves. He licked his lips for the umpteenth time and then smiled broadly into the mirror to be sure his teeth were sparkling clean. He'd purchased a fresh shirt to wear since it was probably the most important day of his life so far. What he will say could possibly end his relationship with Katie, or stabilize it. *God give me the right words.* Ever since he'd heard about her terrible illness, he'd had a dull pit in his stomach. His lovely sweet Katie was dealing with a killer—an ugly destructive element that could change her life forever, as well as shorten it. He was hopeful, since they caught it early, she would one day be free of it. He knew it would lay latent, even if all the signs were missing, but perhaps with all the research going on, there would be a real cure for her type of leukemia long before it might take hold again and cause further anguish.

The news of her possible inability to bear children had been a blow. He had taken Wayne's advice and turned it over to the Lord. At first he was in turmoil, but in time a peace came to him that had to be from above. The thought of adopting kept coming into play and he knew he had enough love to give regardless of the genetics involved. Maybe that was part of God's plan.

Before heading over to the Zook's place, he stopped by to join his family for turkey dinner. There were twenty-six at the extended table and added card tables, most under the age of ten. A pang of sadness soared through him when he realized he might never have his own children to add to the growing family. but that thought quickly left him.

"Pass the *budder* to Josiah," his mother said to one of his young nieces, who was swabbing her warm roll with a glob of butter. "We thought you'd bring Katie by today. Maybe later?"

"Uh, maybe. I'm headed over to see her family when I'm done here."

His father looked at him from the end of the table and nodded. "Thought you two would have set a date by now."

"Well, she's been too busy with her grossmammi."

"How is the dear old lady?" his mother asked.

"I guess she's getting better."

"Ain't you seen her?" his father asked.

"Not for a while. Can someone pass the mashed potatoes?"

The discussion hopped from one subject to another, and several side conversations took place, taking the attention away from Katie and him. He was glad he didn't have to answer any more questions. After an hour or so, the women rose from the table and cleared it while the men remained seated and discussed the wonderful harvest and their plans for the winter. It was difficult to concentrate on anything at this point. Not wanting to appear rude, he waited a few more minutes before excusing himself.

"Josiah, you didn't have dessert yet. We have pumpkin pie."

"I'm too full, Mamm, besides I need to go over to the Zook's."

"I'm sure you'll get your pie, then. Give them my love and if there's time, come back with Katie."

"Jah. Danki." He went over and kissed his mother on the cheek. A couple of his nieces ran over to receive hugs from their favorite uncle and then he departed.

His heart pounded as he approached the drive to the Zook's place. There were several buggies parked in the back.

He removed the harnessing and led his horse to the pasture where all the others were gathered, and then he walked slowly to the back door. He could hear laughter and children's voices as he reached the porch. His first knocks went unheard, so he wrapped louder. Katie's sister, Ruth, opened the door for him. Her eyes widened and her brows rose as she invited him in. Katie was holding one of the twins on her lap, attempting to feed her applesauce. When she saw Josiah standing only ten feet from her, she froze. Applesauce dripped off the spoon onto little Miriam's smock. Ruth reached for her child and Katie stood up, still in shock.

"Hi," was all Josiah was able to say. The family members who were in the kitchen became silent and the air was thick with apprehension.

"Can we go somewhere to talk, Katie?"

Mary was the first to speak. "Happy Thanksgiving, Josiah. We're getting ready to serve dessert. I hope you'll join us."

Katie glared over at her mother. Then she looked back at Josiah and nodded. "I'll get my shawl and we can go in the barn."

"Katie, it's too cold out. Why don't you just go in the dawdi haus. The kinner aren't allowed in there and you can talk better," Mary suggested.

Katie shrugged, removed her shawl from a peg in the kitchen and headed toward the doorway with Josiah following behind. "It's gonna be cold in there, too. I'll need my shawl."

When they walked into the small sitting area, Katie sat on a rocker and waved toward the sofa for Josiah to take a seat. He placed his hat on the floor and leaned forward—his elbows on his knees. "I had to come see you, Katie. Don't be mad."

"I ain't mad." She wrapped her shawl around her arms, shivering slightly from the unheated room.

"I want to talk to you about us," he said, stammering.

"What is there to say? You wrote to me, remember?"

"Jah, but at the time, I didn't know…"

"Know what?" Katie's eyes flashed.

"About your illness, Katie. I had no idea."

"Who told you about me?" Her eyes began to fill. "I didn't want you to know."

"Oh, Katie, why not? I love you. Why wouldn't you let me share this awful thing with you?" He rose and went over to the rocker and stopped it from moving with both hands. Looking down at her troubled face, he wanted so much to hold her and comfort her. She stared up at him, the tears now flowing soundlessly down her cheeks.

"I didn't want you to pity me."

"Katie, Katie. It's not pity I feel. It's sadness and concern. To think you've kept this secret from me all these weeks." He stood up straight and reached for her hands. "Come sit next to me on the sofa, *bitte*."

She complied with his wish and they sat together with only inches between them, though it seemed like a chasm.

"I heard you're improving."

"Becky told you, didn't she?"

"Nee. It was your brudder, but don't be mad at him. He did it because he loves you and he knows we should be together."

"How could he know that? I don't even know if it's true."

"Katie, I know you still love me. You can't deny it."

She wiped her face with her apron and looked down at her lap.

"Well?"

After letting out a long breath, she nodded. "But we can't get married."

"I know why you're saying that."

She looked at him, her mouth dropping.

"Jah, I know about the boppli thing. That you might not be able to have children. It's okay, Katie. I'm not marrying you for kinner. I want to marry you because I love you with all my heart and I won't ever be complete without you in my life. And that's the truth."

She shook her head, as the tears continued to flow unabated. "Every Amish man wants a big family. I've seen you with kinner. You would be a wonderful daed. In time you'd resent me and regret having married me. I can't do that to you."

"Katie, listen to me. Jah, I'd like a family, but if we can't have our own, we can adopt and give other little ones our love. Maybe God wants that for us. He's still in charge you know."

"I don't know what to say, Josiah. My heart is breaking. I want to marry you because I still love you, too, but I don't want to be unfair."

"Then you *have* to marry me, because it would be totally unfair to let me be miserable the rest of my life." He smiled tenderly at her and lifted her chin. "Don't cry, *liebschen*. Please don't." Then he moved closer to her and kissed her salty lips.

Katie began to feel her composure come back. She returned his kiss and placed her arms around his neck. "We don't have to talk about a wedding, Josiah. Let's just wait and see what happens first."

"Nee, we're going to marry as soon as possible. We'll need to publish it and get baptized. I'm glad we took the classes earlier. But we're not waiting any longer. This little cottage will be just fine until you're not needed here to help. It will give me time to finish our house at the same time."

"Josiah, I said some awful things to you—about the house and all. You know I didn't mean them, don't you?"

He grinned and ran his finger along her cheek. "I knew you were just mad like a hornet. I couldn't blame you for that. It didn't look real gut, but you know now I was never unfaithful to you—not even in my head. Ever since I realized I was in love with you, you've been the only woman in my life. I've been so miserable without you."

"I can't believe you're back in my life. It's been so difficult going through all this without you. My family's wonderful, but I still wished you were there for your support. I guess I've been a foolish *maed*. I was just so afraid you'd only stay around because you'd feel too guilty to leave me."

"I understand now. You've been very brave and unselfish, Katie. I guess that's only more reason to love you."

"The doctor didn't say I *couldn't* have children for sure, he just said it can be a problem to get in the family way."

"If you did, would you get sicker?"

"I'd have to give up my medication while I was pregnant, but I could go back on after the delivery."

"During that time, would you get worse?"

"I don't know. There are a lot of things I don't understand about leukemia. I'm still learning about it."

"Would you want to adopt if we can't have our own?"

Katie nodded. "I think so. Nee, I know I would. I love kinner. Until then, I could help at the school house, if I'm no longer needed here at home."

"Katie, we're getting way ahead of ourselves. Let's just enjoy this moment." He moved closer and they held each other in their arms and he whispered sweet talk in their common language and for a short time, Katie and Josiah were able to put every other thought out of their minds, and enjoy each other as they allowed their love to overwhelm them. Then Josiah prayed to God and thanked Him for bringing them together again.

Chapter Thirty-Three
Holmes County, Ohio

That morning, Belinda woke up earlier than usual. It was dark out as she made her way downstairs. Grace was already stuffing two large turkeys. She smiled over at her daughter. "You're up early. Did I make too much noise?"

"Nee. I think I'm just too excited to sleep in. Daed up yet?"

"Oh, jah, he and your brudder are already outside feeding the animals. Want some oatmeal? I made a big pot today."

"I'll have a little. Then I can help you prepare dinner."

"I have to get the turkeys in early. They're big fat ones this year. Over twenty pounds each."

Belinda looked over at the plump pink birds and smiled. I love Thanksgiving. Did you grow enough rutabaga this year?"

"Oh jah. I've been giving it away. Our potatoes were a bumper crop this year, too. Just the right amount of rain and sun. When you're done eating, you can start the sweet potatoes for me."

"Okay. What time are we eating?"

"I told everyone to be here around one. Once everyone arrives, we can sit down to eat. Zeke is coming, you know. We'll seat him next to you."

"Please don't. I don't want to encourage him."

"You could do worse, Belinda. He's a hard worker and a strong Amish man."

"I know. We've been through this before."

"Just don't keep dwelling on what can't be, dochter. It would be a big mistake."

Belinda bit her tongue. The words were dying to spill out, but she would not put a damper on this special day. "Do we have enough brown sugar?"

"In the cupboard. I bought a couple pounds last week."

As Belinda melted butter in a saucepan, Nellie made her appearance. She dipped into the oatmeal and sat at the kitchen table, watching her mother and sister as they prepared for the dinner. "I want to learn to make the creamed onions, Mamm. Can I?"

"You can watch later, but I don't have time to train you this morning. After the holidays, I'll spend more time teaching you. It's never too early to learn."

"Did you bake enough pies, Mamm?"

"Yah, I hope so. I made four apple and four pumpkin."

"That should do it. How many people should we set up for?"

"Last count was twenty. My sister and her family are coming this year. Set up a couple extra places in case I've forgotten someone."

Belinda thought immediately of Jeff and Carrie, but she didn't say a word. She just nodded and after Nellie finished eating, they set up extra card tables and a drop-leaf from the living room, extending the table to seat twenty-five—just in case. They didn't have enough dishes that matched, so it was a colorful display of mismatched china and silverware. For holidays they used real tablecloths and napkins. After they were done,

Belinda and Nellie stepped back to admire their work. "It's pretty, ain't it?" Nellie asked her sister. "Sometimes I wish we had a camera."

"Our minds are like cameras. Just look long and hard and commit it to memory, Nellie. You'd be surprised how that helped me when I was in Pennsylvania. Sometimes I'd lie in bed and picture every one here at home. I could even see the furniture in my head. It was ever so nice."

"You missed us a lot, didn't you?"

"Jah. A lot."

"Now will you miss everyone back in Pennsylvania?"

Belinda laughed. "Probably. Especially the little twins. They are so adorable."

"You and Zeke might have twins. They run in his family."

"Nellie! Not you, too. It's not going to happen. I barely like him."

"You can learn."

"That's not the way it works. Besides, you know who I really like."

"You're making a mistake if you think that will work. You're not even allowed to see him."

Belinda motioned for her sister to enter the pantry with her and when she closed the door, she told her about Jeff and Carrie planning to stop by.

"Whoa! You're gonna get it, Belinda. You'll be grounded for life!"

"They can't do that. I'm nearly eighteen. I'll run off if they try."

Nellie shook her head. "I'm glad I ain't you. I hope there isn't a major scene today."

"Don't tell anyone. Please treat them nice when they come. They won't stay late, but I just have to see Jeff and I'd prefer to do it in public—not like I used to do."

"You'd better pray about it, Belinda. It will take an act of God to make it work."

"Jah, I could use your support, too, Nellie."

"I'm not getting into it. You're on your own."

"Danki! Wait till you need me someday."

"I ain't saying I'll stop loving you. I'm just saying I don't want to be part of your plans. I was once, when you used to sneak out, but that's over."

"Then just say a prayer for things to work out."

"That I can do. We'd better get back and help Mamm now. It's after twelve o'clock."

They went back out and Belinda spooned out fresh cranberry sauce in three separate bowls. Her nerves were in high gear and she perspired, just thinking about what was about to take place. Maybe she should call off Jeff's visit. Before she could finish that thought, she saw the door open and in came Rebecca Smucker along with her four brothers and her parents. Zeke was the first one in the door and he gave a humongous smile. Good grief. What a day this would be.

Lancaster County, Pennsylvania

Katie and Josiah joined the family as they took seats around the long table for dessert. Between Ruth, Emma, and their sisters-in-law, Hannah and Fannie, it wasn't necessary for Katie to leave Josiah's side to help out. They sat, holding hands as they ate with their other hands. Mary looked over at Leroy and beamed. Their Katie was smiling for the first time in weeks. Really smiling, not just a pleasant face put on for her family.

"Have you set a date yet?" Leroy asked the young couple, after they announced that their engagement was on again.

"As soon as we can," Josiah said. "We have to go to the bishop this week and set up our baptisms. I'm glad we took instruction already."

"Jah, that's gut. Will you plan for a wedding this winter?"

"We'll try. Hopefully before Christmas." Josiah squeezed Katie's hand and smiled over at her. "If my bride-to-be agrees."

"Oh, jah. It would be ever so nice."

Oma was settled in her wheelchair at the other end of the table, but when she heard about the wedding plans, she beamed, exposing two gaps on her lower jaw. "I hope I make it until Christmas, then," she said. "Weddings are so wonderful-gut. Especially when it's one of my little nursemaids getting married. Then you can move into that house Josiah's been fixin' up."

"We'll stay here in the dawdi haus until you're strong again, Oma."

Her smile disappeared and a frown took its place. "Mercy, I shouldn't need you to hang around here just to take care of me. Mary's better now."

"And I can help," Wayne said.

"We all can help," Fannie agreed. "Hannah and I will take turns coming over. Whoever stays home will baby-sit."

"I'm such a nuisance." Oma's voice shook.

"Enough of that," Mary said sternly. She turned back to Josiah and Katie. "I'll be able to manage with everyone being so willing to help out."

Ruth and Emma made plans to provide meals a couple times a week. "We can make enough to last two nights. That way you'll have left-overs."

"So you see, Katie, you can move right into your home after the wedding day," Mary said with a giant smile.

Josiah grinned from ear to ear. "I bet this is the happiest day of my life."

Katie giggled. "I hope your wedding day is even better."

"It will be, Katie, I'm certain of that."

"I'm glad I planted extra celery this year," Leroy said. "I figured it wouldn't go to waste. We'll have to make a list and get busy."

"Leroy, you just provide the celery. We ladies will do the rest. I'm getting to be a professional at weddings after planning Ruthie's and Emma's."

"I'm so excited," Katie exclaimed. "I have to pinch myself to know it's real."

"Jah, when I got up this morning, I didn't know if we'd end up together again, or I'd go home the saddest man in Pennsylvania."

Wayne laughed. "If she'd said no, I'd be the unhappiest man in the state. Now I get her room. It's twice the size of mine."

Mary looked at her son. "I don't remember saying we'd move you."

"Golly, I guess I never bothered to tell you," he said.

"I hope Belinda and her family will come back for the wedding," Katie said. "We got close while we worked together.

Oma's eyes brightened. "Oh, jah, my other angel. She'll come, Katie. She wouldn't miss your wedding, I'm sure and certain of that."

"Well, after you talk to the bishop, come back, Josiah, and we'll start talking about plans for the wedding day," Mary added.

"I'll need a new *frack*," Katie said. "I know just the color. I saw the material in Bird-in-Hand last time I was there. "But I'm not telling you, Josiah. I want it to be a surprise."

"Oh, wow, I bet he can hardly wait. Will it be blue? Green? Black? Golly, Josiah, I bet you won't be able to sleep at night." Wayne winked over at his future brother-in-law.

Katie shook her head. "I see I have my brudder back again. I was afraid you'd forgotten how to tease me, Wayne."

"Nee. Never happen." He beamed over at his sister.

That night as Katie tried to sleep, she pictured Josiah's face when she agreed to marry him. He looked like he'd burst. What a fortunate woman she was. In spite of her illness, she was happy. Happier than she'd ever been in her whole entire life. She fell asleep with a smile on her face and a song in her heart. Got is gut.

Chapter Thirty-Four
Holmes County, Ohio

Belinda kept her eyes on the back door. Extended family and close friends appeared throughout the day, and there were at least twenty people around at all times. Zeke seemed to take the hint, and stood with some of the men most of the afternoon, pretty much ignoring her, though she caught him glance over on occasion.

Around four, she heard a car on the drive and knew it was Jeff. Her heart beat wildly as she glanced around to see where her father was. He was returning from the barn with Gideon and Malachi, who was Zeke's younger brother, when the car stopped and Jeff and Carrie emerged. She watched through the window as her father placed his hands on his hips and took a stance. The other men went on toward the house. Then she saw Jeff extend his hand, which was ignored. They stood a few feet apart and she wished she could hear their conversation, but maybe it was just as well she couldn't. Carrie stood several feet back from the men. Belinda couldn't see her face, but her posture was rigid.

After a full five minutes, she watched as Jeff and Carrie retreated to their car. Jeff's body was slumped over. Her father remained standing until the car disappeared from her view. Oh, dear God, he wouldn't even let them come in. Amish were never inhospitable like that. What hope was there for acceptance on the part of her parents? How would this all end? Would they have to elope after-all? Could she abandon her Amish family and community?

Belinda turned and joined her family in the living room. Her heart was heavy, but she'd try however she could to salvage some of the day. It was Thanksgiving Day, after all.

Lancaster County, Pennsylvania

It was all settled. Their baptisms would take place in two weeks. The date for the wedding was set for the Thursday before Christmas and Josiah recruited his family to prepare the house with a final cleaning before the big day. Katie wanted to help, but she was not allowed. Josiah wanted her to take care of herself and rest up for the big day.

During her last doctor's visit, she told everyone on staff about her plans to marry. Even Dr. Humphrey seemed pleased. He was also happy to report that her blood work showed improvement, even though it was slow progress. His nurse hugged her and hinted at wanting an invitation, which Katie extended immediately. The number of guests was already over a hundred and fifty. Esther was coming in from Philadelphia and Belinda had assured her she would be attending, though she couldn't speak for the rest of the family. Jeff's name was not mentioned, leaving Katie to assume things were not going too well on that score, but she hesitated asking over the phone.

Oma was working harder at her therapy and they could see a marked improvement. Nothing like the will to live, to spur on progress. She spent more time on her quilt now, and told Mary she hoped to have it finished by the day of the wedding. When time allowed, Mary pitched in and helped with the quilting, but Katie was no longer allowed near it.

Emma went over to Katie and Josiah's house and helped clean it with Josiah's family. The children behaved well together and Josiah's youngest brother sat on the floor with them and helped them stack blocks. Ruthie sat and held Emma's twins while they napped. Her due date was finally arriving and she was too uncomfortable to clean.

Finally, the wedding day arrived. Katie had trouble sleeping the night before, but she was so excited, it mattered little to her. People arrived early, bringing casseroles, fresh breads and desserts, and platters of meats and cheeses. The festivity was especially well attended as the word spread throughout the Amish community about Katie's illness and her determination to conquer it. She was well-loved by everyone who knew her and her friends showed their delight in her decision to marry. She was showered with gifts and money—even from some of the English who had become her friends during her trial.

Her freshly made dress was a vivid aquamarine, which picked up the color of her eyes. Mary smiled as her daughter donned her frack, as she called her dress, and she took her in her arms. "I'm so happy for you, honey. Josiah is a wonderful man. You will be gut for each other."

"We may try to have a boppli, Mamm. Do you think that's foolish?"

"That has to be your decision, Katie. If it's God's will, then it will happen, but you can't let it ruin your marriage if it doesn't come to pass. You know that."

"We both realize that. We've come to peace with it. We've even come to peace over my illness. We've accepted the fact that no one knows how much time they have on this earth, but it's not the quantity of time, but the quality that's counts. We're going to live each day to the fullest."

"Jah, that's all one can do, Katie. I love you with all my heart, honey. Daed, too. He's so happy that you're getting married to such a gut man. And best of all, we'll be neighbors, nearly. Now let me tuck your hair under your kapp. It's time for you to become a bride. Ready?"

Katie smoothed the front of her dress and smiled at her mother. "I'm ready."

They walked down the stairs to the waiting crowd. There in front stood the man she would share the rest of her life with. Her eyes met Josiah's and she began her journey, wherever it would take her.   *Thank you, Jesus.*

30147243R00162

Made in the USA
Middletown, DE
14 March 2016